Spreadsheets & Sprinkles

Working for Love, Book 3

Amber W. Lynne

Carnelian & Quills

Edited by: Krissy Espindola (KrissyEspindola@gmail.com)
Cover Art by: Rebecca Ruger (BeckandDot@gmail.com)
Paper: ISBN 978-1-960479-29-7
eBook: ISBN 978-1-960479-28-0

Mad Hatter to Alice: "You used to be much more...muchier.
You've lost your muchness."
Tim Burton's 'Alice in Wonderland' 2010

To all the messy women who make the world so much muchier.

Chapter One

Candy

Candy pounded the mound of dough onto the counter, her frustration evident in her grip. The lump of goo hadn't hurt her, but she needed to pound something else, or she'd start looking for someone. Unfortunately, she had no one to blame for her situation but herself.

She loved getting lost in the rhythmic work. Her hands skillfully kneaded a mound of dough with a rhythm born of years of practice. Flour floated in the air like a soft haze, dusting her arms and sweater as she kneaded with a force that wasn't typically required for baking. With each roll and push, her brow furrowed, and she resisted glancing at the bakery's financial ledger, which was open like a chasm on the counter beside her.

Patty's Cakes smelled of sugar, yeast, and a hint of vanilla—except the latter was in short supply. Her supplier had mixed up her last order. Again. Now, she was running out of time to adjust her baking schedule before the morning rush flooded in.

The tinkling bell over the door reset her worry loop. "Melanie! You made it." Candy looked at the clock hanging above the large picture window that faces Main Street. "You're a little late." She dipped her hand into the flour bowl and kept kneading the dough in front of her. "No worries. Can you start on the tarts?"

When Melanie didn't reply, Candy looked up. She stood in the doorway, shoulders rolled forward, fingers tightening around the strap of her apron.

"I'm sorry, Candy," she said, voice thick with guilt. "I can't work for free anymore."

Candy's stomach dropped. "Melanie, it's just a couple more days."

"You said that last week." Her face softened, but her voice didn't waver. "I wanted to tell you in person."

Panic clawed at her ribs. "I'll figure something out, just—"

"No, Candy." Melanie shook of her head, said, "I'm sorry," and then stepped back out the door and disappeared into the flow of early-morning shoppers walking down Main Street.

Candy gripped the counter, her pulse pounding louder than the hum of the fans over the ovens. Patty's Cakes was circling the drain, and she was running out of ways to stop it from taking the final plunge. She yanked her phone from the pocket of her flour-dusted apron and dialed the only number she had memorized.

"I'll be there in—"

"I need help," Candy said as soon as Bailey picked up, pressing her palm to her forehead, hoping to push back the pain gathering there. "Melanie just walked out. I'm drowning in numbers that don't add up. I'm not sure how much longer I can keep this afloat."

"You're ready?"

She hated doing this to her friend, but Candy had run out of options. Bailey had been trying to help her for months. The only thing stopping her from riding in with the cavalry and her family's ridiculous pile of money had been Candy's stubborn refusal of her help.

Now, Bailey's calm voice was a lifeline over the phone. "I was hoping you'd ask for help, and your timing is perfect. That guy I was telling you about, my old friend from high school and, now, accountant, is in town visiting his folks."

"An accountant? I was thinking more along the lines of you throwing on an apron and coming here to help man the shop."

"Candice Linn Brinley, you can't keep hiding from your problems."

"Bailey Ray Reynolds, don't you dare first, middle, and last name me."

"You know I'm right." Bailey sighed into the phone. "Things at the café have only been getting worse. I think he can help you."

"Maybe."

"You asked for help."

"A different type of help."

"You don't get to be picky about help, and you know the only help I can offer. These nails aren't made for piping bags."

Candy looked at the pile of dough that was forming a film and drying out. "I know. It's just really hard. My mom did this—"

"Alone, and you aren't alone. This has been going on for…I don't know…too long. When I heard he was coming, I was actually hoping you could meet."

"So, you were preparing to ambush me?"

"Overreacting much? Please." Bailey let out a long sigh. "I bet he could make sense of your books. Let me bring him by Patty's Cakes later. You'll love him. He likes spreadsheets, and he's got a knack for making things like this better."

"I need hands to help with things here, not math solutions."

"Fixing your finances *is* fixing the bakery." Bailey's voice softened. "Candy, you can't keep doing this on your own."

She didn't have time for emotions. Instead, she exhaled sharply and rubbed at her temple, smudging more flour across her face. "Fine."

"Fine?" Bailey asked, surprised.

"Fine," Candy repeated, defeated. "But if I don't like him, he's gone."

"You'll like him," Bailey said confidently. "I'll text when we're on our way."

Candy hung up, staring at her phone as if it had betrayed her. She still needed help with the baking, and now she was letting a stranger dig through the wreckage of her books. Maybe this was just another crappy decision, but it couldn't make things worse, right?

Or maybe—perhaps—he could keep things from falling apart before they crushed her.

She turned back to her dough, rolling her sleeves up higher. It didn't matter who was coming. She needed to keep moving.

Mumbling to herself, she started kneading. "Patty's Cakes isn't going to save itself."

The bell above the door jingled again, and Candy looked up, expecting Bailey, but not the man standing beside her. He did *not* belong at Patty's Cakes. His broad shoulders and narrow waist looked like he hadn't eaten a pastry in his entire life.

Bailey flashed her a knowing grin. "Candy, meet Lincoln. Lincoln, this is Candy."

Candy's stomach clenched. He was tall, lean, and sharply dressed. A stark contrast to the flour-covered chaos she was experiencing. He looked neat. Precise. Organized. He radiated common sense and stability.

Lincoln extended his hand. "Nice to meet you. Bailey tells me you could use some help."

Candy eyed the hand warily before wiping hers on her apron and shaking it. "Some. I'm really fine. We're just a little short-staffed, short on vanilla, and short on…"

She shifted to turn back to her dough, misjudging the motion entirely, and before she could stop it—

Poof.

A violent cloud of flour exploded into the air, cascading down onto Lincoln's perfectly pressed suit.

Her mouth parted in horror.

Lincoln coughed once, then again, and then—without breaking expression—he calmly took off his glasses, wiped them with a precision she'd never learned to master, and placed them back onto his face.

Bailey pressed her lips together, failing miserably at hiding her glee.

Candy dropped the rolling pin and grabbed a towel, launching forward. "Oh my gosh! I am so sorry!"

He held up a hand as if to stop her from making the situation so much worse. "It's fine." His tone was measured. "Accidents happen."

Candy stopped dead, gripping the towel. "You sound like you get flour dumped on you all the time."

He said, "I don't."

Bailey clapped her hands together. "Well. This went well."

Candy still wanted to crawl into the nearest pastry display and never return. "Look, I know Bailey thinks you can help, but I—"

Lincoln's eyes flickered toward the half-open ledger. Even from a distance, even *covered in flour*, he seemed to see something in the mess of numbers that Candy had been dreading for months. His gaze was sharp, assessing. Calculating.

There was a long pause. Then, finally, he looked at her again. "You love this place."

Candy blinked. "Of course I do."

"Then let me help you keep it."

She wanted to say *no* out of instinct. Wanted to pretend she wasn't struggling as she watched her mother's business fall apart. Except...she was.

"Okay," she muttered.

Lincoln nodded. "I'll need full access to your records and receipts. And—"

Candy sighed. "Oh, this is going to be...so much fun."

Bailey bit back a laugh, and Lincoln—*stoic, flour-covered Lincoln*—stepped farther into Patty's Cakes, scanning the space like he already knew all the areas that weren't working.

Candy swore she saw the very *second* that he realized just how much trouble she was really in.

Yeah. This was going to be a disaster.

Chapter Two

Candy

"That's all I've got," said Candy, as she folded her arms and leaned against the counter, doing her best to look unimpressed as her new accountant shuffled through a thick folder of receipts and invoices. His clean fingers flipped through each page methodically, his forehead creasing deeper with every passing second, and, now and then, he would let out a quiet sigh...small, controlled, but still thoroughly irritated.

She shouldn't find that satisfying. Oh, but she did. Yes, it was *her* mess, but it wasn't due to a lack of effort trying to make it work. If he couldn't see that—

"You do realize this is..." He lifted a few papers and tilted them toward her. "...a disaster."

Candy straightened, lifting her chin. "It's a system."

"No, it's not."

"Yes, it's like..." She waved her hands around, trying to find the right words. "...organized chaos."

"It's only one of those things." He pulled out a receipt and held it up. "Did you know you've been paying double for flour deliveries for the last six months?"

She opened her mouth to reply, but no words came out. She snatched the paper and looked at the line item. The numbers on the page blurred in front of her, but they didn't lie. The price was nearly twice what it should have been. Her stomach clenched.

"This—this has to be a mistake," she muttered.

Lincoln didn't press her; instead, he turned to another sheet, his expression unreadable. "And here, your supplier billed you for twenty pounds of butter that your inventory doesn't show you received. Did you catch that one?"

She swallowed. "I—" Her stomach twisted—because there, in black-and-white, was proof of something she hadn't noticed at all.

His silence was both expectant and damning.

"Look, I don't need you to state the obvious. I'm well aware things aren't perfect, but—"

"Candy. We've been at this for two days." Lincoln's voice was calm. He clipped the receipts together in one neat motion before setting them down. "This paints a clear picture. If you continue like this, Patty's Cakes won't survive another three months."

She fought the urge to push away the receipts—and him and his warnings. She had spent months telling herself that if she just worked harder, sold more, and kept things going, things would turn around. But they weren't turning. Instead, they were unraveling faster.

She pulled away from the counter, brushing past him

toward the sink, scrubbing nonexistent flour from her hands—anything—to stay grounded. The truth was too overwhelming, pressing against her ribs. "I don't need you to state the obvious."

"I didn't think I had to," Lincoln said simply.

Panic flared, a visceral reaction she barely swallowed down. Candy squeezed her eyes shut.

She wasn't ready to face all of this with him...not yet.

"I have to go," she murmured, wiping her hands aggressively on a kitchen towel before grabbing her coat.

Lincoln's eyes narrowed. "Go where? We've barely gotten started."

"I just—I need some air," she said too quickly. She gestured vaguely at the haphazard pile of oil-stained receipts, delivery slips, and payroll stubs littering her butcher block counter. "You need time to look through all of *that* anyway."

"Yes, but I need you here in case I have questions."

"And you'll get answers...in twenty minutes."

"Candy." His hand shifted as if he was about to reach for her, but stopped his hand in midair.

She recoiled before he could finish. "Don't."

Something flickered in his expression then—only for a second—but she caught it. Not frustration. Not impatience. Something quieter.

She looked away before it settled. "Just...a little time." Then, before he could say anything else, she yanked open the door and slipped out.

Candy sat down on her mother's small bed. Her fingers subconsciously traced the pastel quilt she had brought from their home when she'd moved Patty into the assisted living facility in Serenity.

The room was simple, cluttered with old cookbooks and a framed photograph of Patty's Cakes in its early days. It was a black-and-white image with the grand opening ribbon still taut, crisp, and new.

"Mama..." Candy hesitated, her voice barely above a whisper. "What would you do?"

Patricia Brinley sat across from her, wrapped in a cardigan that looked too big for her shrinking frame. She blinked as if sorting through her words before she fully understood them. Some days were like that. Her mother had never been slow or uncertain. Now, Candy wasn't sure if today was a good day or a bad one.

"What would I do about what, sweetheart?" her mother finally asked, her tone as gentle as it had always been.

Candy exhaled, staring down at her hands. "The bakery. It's..." Her throat went tight. "It's bad, Mom."

Her mother sighed, eyes briefly slipping to the window. For a moment, Candy thought she might not answer.

"Patty's Cakes has always been about more than recipes and numbers, you know that."

"Yeah, but the numbers pay the bills." Candy laughed, shaking her head. "And right now, mine are a total disaster."

Patty's fingers toyed with the hem of her cardigan. Then, in a voice so soft, so certain, she said, "Have you found what makes the Patty cake special?"

Candy frowned. "Special?"

"The thing that makes it more than just flour and sugar," her mother said, as if it were obvious. "It was never just a recipe, sweetheart."

"Mom…" Candy's frustration swelled, hot and sudden. Not at her mother, not at the fragile mind she was losing in pieces, but at the universe, at time itself, at the helplessness she felt. Her mother's dementia had only gotten worse in recent months. Candy felt like her world was falling apart. First it was her mother, and now the bakery.

Candy sighed and reached out for her mother's hand, giving it a gentle squeeze. It was warm, familiar, and comforting—even if the woman holding it was no longer fully present. The steady hum of conversation and soft music filled the hall outside her mother's small room, but Candy felt like she was in a quiet bubble, alone except for the one person she could always talk to, even if she wasn't sure her words would be heard.

"I don't know if I can fix it, Mama," she admitted, her voice coming out quieter than she meant. "The bakery…it's worse than I thought. I've been trying so hard, but I keep messing up."

Her mother hummed, a faint sound of understanding.

"And—and Bailey brought someone in to help. A numbers guy." Candy paused, saying his name out loud for the first time like this. "Lincoln."

Her mother's lips curled just slightly.

"He's practical," Candy continued, "smart, and honestly? He's already noticing everything I shouldn't have missed."

Her mother's fingers—warm and familiar—squeezed hers back.

Candy swallowed. "It's humiliating realizing how bad things are. That I've let it get like this." A hollow laugh slipped out. "And, I don't even know if he can fix it."

The breath she released loosened the ache just a fraction. She wasn't expecting answers, and she knew her mother couldn't offer solutions, but she wanted to say it out loud...to step out of fear and into something else.

A beat of silence passed between them. Then, her mother gave her hand another gentle squeeze. "You're a good girl," Patty murmured, her eyes momentarily clearer than before.

She hadn't expected an answer. She knew her mother couldn't offer solutions. Certainly not in the way she needed, but being here, in this quiet moment, was enough.

Even if it still felt like she was grasping at pieces of a life that was changing too fast, slipping between her fingers no matter how hard she fought. She bit her lip, blinking rapidly.

She wasn't ready for any of this, and she wasn't sure if she ever would be.

Chapter Three

Lincoln

The small office tucked in the back of Patty's Cakes was a disaster zone.

Lincoln crossed his arms, examining the chaos across the desk. Crumpled receipts, piles of invoices with scribbled notes in the margins, and an open ledger that looked barely touched. This wasn't just messy bookkeeping; it was a paper avalanche waiting to happen.

He exhaled slowly, adjusting his glasses as he reached for the nearest receipt.

Flour-streaked. Smudged ink. Barely legible. And yet...he frowned, tilting it toward the warm glow of the desk lamp.

$42.50 (Farmer's Market Apples. Mrs. Danvers loves the Honeycrisp tarts. Remember to set two aside for her next week.)

Lincoln blinked. That wasn't a normal business note. He set it aside and grabbed another.

$18.75 (Pecans. Henry swears the new batch is fresher. Test for next Tuesday's pies.)

His brow furrowed. He flipped to the next.

$63.00 (Custom Cake for Jasmine's 8th Birthday. Add extra butterflies per her request. She's obsessed with purple this month!)

A deep crease formed between his brows. Lincoln combed through more receipts, more invoice notes, more slips of paper that should have been nothing more than functional financial records, but, instead, they read like…like *stories*.

Tiny, detailed snapshots of people who exist in Candy's world. People she kept track of, not just as customers, but as…*hers*.

Lincoln set them down slowly, rubbing a tired hand along the scruff of his jaw.

This? *This* was why the bakery was in trouble.

It wasn't just disorganization. It was her *heart* bleeding into business, and unfortunately, her heart didn't pay the bills. It didn't keep supply orders from getting muddled. It didn't prevent financial disaster from creeping up like a slow-burning fire. But it also wasn't something Lincoln could easily ignore.

He sighed, leaning back in his chair, eyes scanning the scattered remnants of Candy's world. The way she managed Patty's Cakes wasn't about profit margins or growth expansion. It was about *people*.

And as much as he wanted to criticize this system—the complete lack of a sustainable structure—he couldn't overlook the small details. The doodles in the corners of handwritten recipe sheets, tiny sketches of flowers and smiling cupcakes, and the way she left post-it notes in cursive, reminding herself to check on a customer's recovering grandmother.

The business wasn't inefficient because she was careless. It was because Candy didn't separate Patty's Cakes from herself. He was beginning to realize that, maybe, that was what made it special.

His phone buzzed on the desk, breaking through the silence. Lincoln picked it up, reading the text on the screen.

Are you in town yet? Your father wants help sorting through the garage when you get a chance.

He hovered his thumb over the screen before typing a response.

Hey Mom. Taking care of business. Be there soon.

His finger hesitated over the send button. Was this 'taking care of business'? That's all this was, right? A job. A favor. Some routine accounting cleanup before he packed up, helped his parents move, and returned back to...*whatever came next.*

Lincoln exhaled and pressed send.

He stared at it longer than needed, feeling...wrong. Maybe this wasn't just a job, and he was beginning to care more than he should.

The faint chime of the front door caught his attention. Lincoln glanced up through the small glass window of the office, his focus shifting to the bakery entrance.

Candy stood in the doorway, rubbing her arms, her face partially shadowed under the dim glow of the shop's warm lighting. She looked...different. Not the whirlwind of energy she'd been that morning with flour-dusted cheeks and a playful bite to her words.

She looked tired.

Something in Lincoln's chest twisted suddenly. Without hesitation, his fingers gripped the scattered receipts on the desk.

The fragile papers, the chaotic notes, the heart stitched into every single detail.

He wanted to fix this. Not because it was his job. Not because of numbers, but because it was *her*. Lincoln inhaled slowly, releasing his grip on the papers.

They needed to figure out how to save Patty's Cakes, but first, he'd have to figure out exactly how to make sure this kept feeling like business and not...something more.

Chapter Four

Candy

When Candy stepped back into the bakery, a fragrant wall of warm berry tarts and sugar wrapped around her like a familiar hug, but it didn't bring the same comfort as it usually did.

She had been gone longer than she had promised Lincoln, and sure enough, when she reentered the kitchen, she found him exactly where she had left him—except now, her messy pile of receipts and invoices had been organized into neat, methodical stacks.

He looked up as she walked in, his expression unreadable.

"That was twenty minutes?" he asked, one brow lifting.

Candy exhaled, scrubbing a hand over her face. "It was...rounded up."

Lincoln rearranged his papers before flipping through a stack of receipts. "Candy, these numbers, they aren't right. There's something wrong here."

"I'm sorry. Clearly, I'm better at baking than I am at math." She let out a sigh, the exhaustion of the last few months pressing against her chest again. "You've been saying that since you walked in."

"Because it's true." Lincoln straightened from the counter and reached for a notebook, flipping it open. He held up two pages side by side—one with her current financial records and the other, a breakdown of her monthly expenses. "Your supply costs spiked three months ago. Ingredients you've been getting from the same vendors for years had their prices double overnight."

She frowned, stepping closer. "So? Prices go up. Inflation *is* a thing."

"This isn't normal inflation." He pointed to a column, his voice measured but firm. "Candy, someone's been making purchases under your business account that don't add up. It's not just the butter. Your supplier also billed you for ten gallons of milk you never received. And flour—" He flipped to another receipt. "You've never gone through a hundred pounds a month of flour. You're paying for more than what's being delivered."

Candy stiffened. "That has to be a mistake."

"Is it?" he countered, arching a brow. "Because judging by these reports, if the missing funds had actually stayed in the bakery, you might actually be thriving right now." He looked around the room, and his eyes went down towards his stack of receipts. "Despite your 'unique' filing system."

A cold chill ran through her. No. No way. She would've noticed. She would have—but she hadn't.

He was...helping. Still, admitting that felt like swallowing glass. Would she have noticed any of this without Lincoln? No, and maybe she was a little bit pissed about that.

He paused. Lincoln's fingers tightened around an invoice; his expression was unreadable. "Candy," he said slowly. "Who's Bradley?"

Her stomach twisted at the name. "What?"

Lincoln turned the invoice toward her. "Bradley Tate. His name is all over these supplier orders."

The breath stalled in Candy's lungs. She met his gaze, but his intensity made her shift uncomfortably. "He—he used to handle orders," she admitted, running a flour-dusted hand over her apron. "He was involved in the business. A while ago."

Lincoln watched her explain, then lowered the page. "Involved how?"

She hesitated. She could lie or play it off like it wasn't a big deal. But Lincoln was sharp—too sharp. If she even tried, he'd see right through her.

Candy braced herself. "He was my boyfriend."

Lincoln didn't react—even his expression stayed perfectly neutral. He just nodded once, setting the invoice neatly on top of the others. "And he managed the finances?"

Candy shifted her weight and said, "At the time, yeah. He wanted to, and he said it made sense to streamline things." She swallowed, forcing herself to add the part that burned the most. "He said he wanted to help make things easier for me. I trusted him."

Lincoln was silent longer than she liked. He didn't have to say anything for the implications to slam into her all at once.

Her business was failing, and it looked like it wasn't *actually* her fault. At least not intentionally.

The truth hit hard. Bradley had left because she was a mess.

He'd argued that he was doing everything, and she couldn't get it together, but he'd been undermining her the whole time. Her inability to see that hadn't just cost her a relationship. It might have cost her *everything*.

Lincoln was silent long enough for unease to crawl under her skin. Then he said, "Why did you break up?"

Candy stiffened. "What does that have to do with anything?"

"Because whoever was handling these accounts didn't just mismanage things," he said evenly. "They let them spiral into disaster. Which means they either walked away from a mess...or *created* it. And based on what I'm seeing," Lincoln lifted the file slightly, tapping a finger against the numbers, "I need to know if this was negligence or intent."

Candy's breath hitched, and her fingers flexed.

She wanted to argue and tell Lincoln he was wrong. Bradley wouldn't have done something like this. Whatever had happened with the books, it had to be an accident, but had she been looking at them back then? *Really* looking?

No.

Bradley had handled invoices and supply accounts willingly. He had insisted on taking over the money when Candy was overwhelmed with her mother's health. Her shoulders felt tight just thinking about those late nights, and Bradley gently coaxing her away from worrying about the bakery's books.

"Just let me help, Candy. You've got enough on your plate."

He'd known she was distracted. He'd known she wasn't keeping track, and then, just when things started to slip and she *had* begun noticing vendor mistakes and missing costs, Bradley was gone.

Her stomach twisted.

Lincoln's voice was quiet. "Candy."

She swallowed hard. "He wasn't—" She let out a breath. "He *isn't* some kind of thief, okay? I mean, he was trying to help."

Lincoln's brow twitched slightly, but he didn't argue.

Instead, with an unsettling calm, he asked, "You trusted him. Did he trust you?"

The question hit deeper than she'd like.

Candy looked away, her hands fisting tighter. Their breakup hadn't been dramatic. There'd been no shouting fights and no big revelations. Bradley had looked at her one day, exhausted and exasperated and...done.

"You don't take anything seriously, Candy."

"Is this all you can do?"

"I can't keep doing this—cleaning up after your chaos."

And she'd felt sorry for him. Sorry, he was stuck with her.

Candy slowly exhaled, opening her eyes. She turned back to Lincoln, her voice quieter now. "We broke up because I wasn't what he needed," she said. "He wanted someone organized. Someone structured. I wasn't enough of those things."

There was no hard logic, no immediate analysis, or sharp response. Just silence. Then, softer than she expected, he asked, "And what did *you* need?"

She squeezed her eyes shut. How ironic.

For so long, she'd thought *she* was the reason their partnership—both in business and in life—had fallen apart. *Her* messy way of doing things. *Her* instinctive approach. But now, standing in the middle of her crumbling bakery, she had a horrifying thought.

What if Bradley hadn't left because she was failing?

What if he'd needed her to believe that so she wouldn't look too closely?

Her pulse quickened.

"I would have noticed," she murmured, her confidence faltering.

Lincoln didn't look convinced.

"Candy," he said, softer now, "numbers don't lie."

Her throat tightened.

She didn't want to believe it, but deep down, she already knew. Bradley had hurt her before. She just never thought—never imagined—he could stoop *this* low.

"I—" Candy pressed a hand against her temple, her thoughts spinning. "So, what am I supposed to do? March up and ask him if he stole from me?"

Lincoln didn't blink. "No. You fix this. Properly."

A bitter laugh bubbled up her throat. "Oh, great. Let me just pull a magic fix-it recipe out of my apron. Problem solved."

"You need a solution," Lincoln pressed. "Fast. Revenue is down, your budget is already stretched, and even if we cut unnecessary expenses, it won't be enough. You need new cash flow, immediately."

Candy rubbed at a headache forming at her temples. They needed a creative solution — and fast.

That's when it hit her. Her eyes snapped open. "Sweet Success," she blurted.

Lincoln frowned. "What?"

"The Sweet Success baking contest," she rushed to the desk in the corner. "Mom always talked about entering, but she never had time. It's got big prize money — more than enough. If I enter, and if I win..."

Somewhere in the chaos was what she needed. Candy yanked open drawer after drawer in her mother's old desk, pushing past crumpled menus, scattered coupons, and a rolling pin that definitely didn't belong there.

Lincoln leaned against the door, arms crossed, watching her with an expression that mixed mild amusement and deep regret. "Is this a normal way for you to find things, or am I just lucky enough to witness it firsthand?"

"This," said Candy, as she huffed and pushed aside a tangle of old ribbons, "is a very sophisticated organizational system."

"I see."

She appeared to ignore the clear skepticism in his tone and let out a triumphant sound as her fingers finally grasped a bright pink flyer. Straightening up, she smoothed it out between them, tapping the bold title at the top. *Sweet Success Baking Competition.*

"That's your solution?" Lincoln stated flatly. "A contest?"

Candy gestured dramatically. "A contest with a cash prize!"

Lincoln's gaze barely flickered as he read over the details while Candy watched him excitedly. "Twenty thousand dollars," he murmured, eyes scanning the fine print.

"Enough to give Patty's Cakes a fighting chance," she

confirmed. "Enough to keep things stable while we fix what Bradley—" Her voice caught, but she pressed on. "While we undo the damage that's been done."

Lincoln's brows lifted.

"You just said I need money." Her hand tightened. "Well, this is how I can get it."

I meant like borrowing from Bailey or getting a small loan to resolve this delivery billing issue." He exhaled, shaking his head as if he couldn't believe what she was saying. "Candy, what are the chances of winning this contest?"

"We have to do something, right?" she snapped, her pulse hammering. "Mom had always talked about entering. Maybe this is my shot at saving this place. Doing something, she never did. It would be a way of making a Patty cake that's all mine."

Lincoln rubbed his hand down his face. "Candy, do you realize how unbelievably risky that is?" He looked at her, and for a moment, she thought he might understand that edge of desperation beneath the surface. But then, just as fast, the skepticism came back.

"You really think that's a solid financial strategy? Entering a contest wasn't a recommended course of action for these circumstances when I was training to get my MBA."

"This is my shot."

"Maybe."

"It's better than sitting here crying over Bradley." Her voice cracked despite herself. "You already said it, Lincoln. I have to fix it. So, let me fix it."

Her words settled between them like the flour dusting the counter.

Finally, Lincoln sighed. Something flickered behind his expression, maybe reluctant admiration, maybe exasperation—but when he shook his head, the corner of his mouth almost lifted.

"This might be the worst idea I've ever agreed to," he muttered, pulling his hands down his face. "You don't win just because you want to."

"And you don't win if you don't try," Candy shot back.

Something in the air shifted between them. For a long moment, Lincoln just stared at her. Then, finally, he sighed.

Candy lit up. "So, that's a, yes?"

"It's a very cautious yes," Lincoln corrected, shooting her a pointed look. "If we're doing this, we're doing it the right way. No cutting corners. No guessing. We plan, prepare, and strategize."

"Sure, sure," Candy said quickly. "Strategy. Plans. Whatever you say."

Lincoln gave her a long, exhausted look.

Candy grinned, something fierce sparking inside her. Bradley thought he had already won, but he had *no* idea what was coming.

Chapter Five

Lincoln

"So, we start now." Lincoln set the flyer down and clasped his hands in front of him. "If you really want this, we need a plan. Convince me."

Candy blinked. "What?"

"You heard me. Show me how this will work." He studied her carefully. "Why you? What's your edge? What's going to make you stand out from the other numerous hopefuls that I am sure are entering?"

Squaring her shoulders, she leaned forward. "First of all, Patty's Cakes has always been known for its baking. My mother never entered, but she could have. People still talk about her patty cake." She crossed her arms. "And, in a competition like this, story matters. The last few winners had sentimental ties to their recipes. One was a family bread passed down for generations, the other used honey from her late grandfather's apiary. The judges eat that stuff up."

"Sentiment doesn't pay bills."

"No, but presentation does," Candy argued. "The recipe itself *is* the edge. Nobody else has my mother's formula."

Lincoln held back, then said, "Right. But what's stopping someone else from having something *better*?"

"I'm stopping them," she shot back. "Because my version isn't just about following a formula—it's about making something real. Something people love. The judges want a story, but they also want something undeniably good." She tipped her chin up. "And that's exactly what I'm going to give them."

Lincoln exhaled, rubbing his jaw. "Alright. What about the competition? Who else is entering?"

Candy hesitated, but only for a second. "I-I don't know yet."

His gaze sharpened. "Knowing what we're up against would help."

She shifted under his scrutiny but refused to shrink away from it. "Fine. Then we do our homework. We prep, we test, and we don't second-guess."

Lincoln studied her. She was...cute...like a flour-dusted fairy when she was excited. Finally, he reached for the flyer, again, scanning the schedule. "How much time do we have?"

Candy's pulse kicked up. "Three weeks."

"Less than a month."

"Plenty of time."

"That's *no* time," he countered. "You have a disorganized business, a skeleton crew staff, and based on what I've observed, your process consists of gut instinct and wishful thinking."

Candy crossed her arms. "Ah, so now we've gone from 'guesswork' to 'wishful thinking.' Good to know."

"Do you even have a test schedule set up? Ingredient sourcing? A practice timeline?"

She waved a hand. "I work intuitively."

Lincoln stared at her. "*That* doesn't win competitions."

Candy huffed. "So, what, you think I can't do this?"

"I think entering without a plan is reckless."

She rolled her eyes. "If we had more time, would you still think this was a bad idea?"

"Contests are a fine marketing strategy for a thriving business, but" Lincoln hesitated. "...if we had six months, maybe."

Then we'll create a two-week plan," she said quickly. "You mentioned we need structure, right? Great. You handle the strategy, analyze the numbers, manage your calendar and budget, and *I'll* take care of the actual baking. Just let me *do this*."

Lincoln exhaled, rubbing his jaw as he mulled it over. He hated this idea. He really, really hated this idea.

But despite himself, he could see the logic in it. The bakery needed cash quickly, and if this wasn't the answer, he honestly didn't have a better option, nothing besides leveraged debt. Anything less than a large influx of cash wouldn't suffice. "What about that loan? Bailey—"

"Has her own problems, and I don't want her rescuing me."

"Bailey wouldn't consider it rescuing. I think she'd call it helping."

"I need to know I can do this on my own." Candy traced a finger in the flour on the table in front of her. "What if all of this is falling apart because of me?"

He ran a final glance over the flyer, then looked back at Candy, who was shifting her weight from foot to foot like she was bracing herself for him to shut this down completely, but her eyes—determined and hopeful—were locked onto his.

"Fine." He let out a long, slow sigh. "But talk to Bailey, too, so she can be ready to bail you out if this wild plan doesn't work."

Candy straightened. "Fine?"

Lincoln gave her a withering look. "Regrettably, yes."

With wide arms and a cheerful smile, she made a move toward him before hesitating, then grabbed an apron from the hook by the register. She returned to where he stood and hung it around his neck with a satisfied little tug. "Welcome to Patty's Cakes. We're grateful for your service."

Lincoln muttered something about questionable career choices, but Candy swore, as he flipped the flyer over to review the contest rules, the corner of his lip almost—almost—twitched.

Now, he stood in the middle of Candy's kitchen, trying not to blink too often at the chaos that had somehow been turned into a workspace. Flour was spread unevenly across the counters, half-measured ingredients lay like breadcrumbs for a recipe only she could understand, and a scatter of sticky notes peppered every surface not already covered in clutter.

He handed over a color-coded planning sheet in a laminated pocket.

She blinked at it like it might bite.

"You color-coded the schedule?"

He adjusted his glasses. *Of course, he had.* "It's efficient."

She flipped the paper in her hands. "It's excessive."

"It's necessary." His voice was steady, but he was already tallying the inefficiencies around the room.

She didn't give him time to list off the results of his chaos audit. Instead, Candy let out a sigh so performative that it practically arrived with stage lights. "I *do* have structure."

Lincoln didn't move from his spot. He folded his arms neatly, with a rising bemusement. The anxiety he always seemed to manage around her was eased only by the growing realization that nothing in this room — not her techniques, ingredients, or scribbles — followed any system he recognized.

Your 'structure' includes three different flavor variations scribbled on napkins, a sticky note that says, 'sprinkle love in every recipe,' and a supply list riddled with more question marks than actual numbers. He gave her the flattest look he could manage. "Forgive me if I don't find that reassuring."

She didn't flinch. If anything, her chin rose in defiance.

"Sprinkle love is an essential step in baking," she declared.

That part unnerved him more than the dough crusted onto the side of the fridge. Mainly, because he knew she believed it.

"That's not an ingredient," he said, trying for patience, but her expression—wide-eyed indignation, full tilt charm—nearly cracked his resolve.

"You take that back right now!"

He rolled his eyes. It probably said something about him that he found this woman—who ran her kitchen like a cross between a carnival and a crisis—entirely impossible, and deeply compelling.

"This is going to be a long three weeks."

Just then, the door swung open, and Bailey breezed into the culinary war zone, armed with coffee and the strappiest sandals that left her feet nearly bare. She apparently had no concern for kitchen health codes.

"Oh no, don't let me interrupt," she said, grinning around a sip. "This is the best entertainment I've had all week."

Lincoln glanced her way, deadpan. "Did she call you in to double-team me?"

"Moral support," Bailey said sweetly.

Lincoln dragged a chair over to the counter and sat down, already revising the production timeline in his head. The mission was simple on paper: prepare Candy for Sweet Success, fix the bakery's systems where possible, and keep emotional entanglement to a minimum. But that was before he realized just how chaotic—fiercely, fearlessly unstructured—Candy's world really was. Or, how much he didn't hate being in it.

He cleared his throat and refocused. "Alright, let's try this again. If we want to win Sweet Success, we need to balance creativity with precision."

Candy flopped dramatically onto a stool, chin in her palm. "Precision makes me itchy."

Bailey shrugged, "She's not lying. I've seen it."

"That explains a lot." Lincoln glanced sideways, holding back the smile threatening to form at the corner of his mouth. "She's your friend, and you're the last line of defense if this doesn't work."

"It'll work," said Candy with a glare.

He watched the two women whisper and giggle while he

breathed through the tension in his shoulders. Numbers, rules, frameworks—those were his language. This? This was something else entirely. Baking with intent, but no pattern. Leading with instinct. Operating by feel rather than formula. It was frustrating.

It was also...kind of fascinating.

He sighed.

Three weeks had never felt so long, or so strangely worth it.

Chapter Six

Candy

The kitchen was filled with the aroma of melted butter, vanilla, and a hint of citrus zest. Candy moved swiftly, her hands working effortlessly as she measured, poured, and mixed. Across from her, Lincoln sat at the counter, precise as ever, flipping through a leather-bound planner, each movement deliberate, his focus unwavering.

"You know," she said, cracking an egg against the side of the bowl, "you're taking this 'strategy' thing way too seriously."

Lincoln didn't look up. "Strategy is the difference between success and disaster."

Candy scoffed. She *almost* felt bad for him. "This is a baking competition, not a corporate takeover."

Finally, Lincoln lifted his gaze and gave her one of his signature unimpressed looks. "Tell me again how well spontaneity has served your finances?"

She opened her mouth to argue...then closed it. Instead, she sighed dramatically and flicked a bit of flour toward him.

"Rude. If you're just going to judge me, you might as well test your own theories."

Lincoln frowned. "I *am* testing them--through you."

Candy smirked and tapped the wooden spoon against the edge of the bowl. "Nope. Hands-on experience is the best way to learn. Grab your apron, genius."

Lincoln glanced at the flour-covered counter. Then at her. Then back at the counter. "Absolutely not."

"You afraid of a little flour?" she taunted, hands on her hips.

A muscle twitched in his jaw. Then, with a resigned exhale, he reached for the apron, eyeing it as if it were a wildly foreign artifact.

Before he could overthink it, Candy reached over to help adjust the strings at his waist. "You tie it like this." Their hands brushed, and for the briefest moment, she forgot how to breathe. His hands were firm, strong, but soft.

Judging by the way Lincoln stiffened slightly, she wasn't the only one who noticed.

Lincoln folded his arms. "And what *exactly* am I supposed to be doing?"

Candy grinned mischievously. "Piping frosting. Ever decorated a cupcake before?"

"I feel like you already know the answer."

Undeterred, she handed him a piping bag. He held it as if it might burst open to fling frosting all over him.

"Relax," she teased. "It's not a bomb."

Lincoln took a deep breath and gave it a firm squeeze, sending a lopsided glob of frosting onto the counter instead of the cupcake.

"Steady, cowboy!" Candy wheezed. "Don't rush."

Lincoln's expression was pure exasperation. "It was a test squeeze."

"It's okay, it happens to a lot of first timers." Candy wiped at her eyes, laughing.

Lincoln tried again. This time, the frosting mostly landed on the cupcake...kind of. The swirl looked sad. Slumped. Defeated.

She leaned in, her shoulder bumping his. "You are truly terrible at this," she whispered conspiratorially.

Lincoln sighed. "Well, I was busy learning how to read actuary tables instead of adding 'pastry chef' to my resumé."

Her shoulders shook. "Okay, okay—here. Let me help."

She wasn't thinking when she did it—she wasn't considering how close they were, how his warm hand fit underneath hers, or how she could sense the controlled tension in his arm as he adjusted his grip.

Candy reached over him, guiding his hand down the tube of frosting. "See?" she murmured, positioning the piping bag gently between their fingers. "It's all in the pressure. Steady, controlled..."

She wasn't thinking about how close they were, or how warm his hand was beneath hers. Or how, when she turned her head ever so slightly, their faces were just a breath apart.

Lincoln wasn't pulling away. In fact, *he wasn't moving at all.* He wasn't looking at the cupcake. He was looking at her.

The air between them shifted, subtle, but unmistakable. The playful rhythm stilled, and something quieter settled in its place. Closer. Warmer.

Her pulse lurched, and her breath caught before she could disguise it. The silence held, thick with an edge she hadn't felt just moments ago.

His gaze lingered, not searching...settling. As if he were memorizing the lines of her face. The air around them had grown suddenly charged.

She forced her hand to move slowly away, brushing flour from the inside of her wrist, and stepping back just enough to break the pull of tension that had ignited between their bodies. Her fingertips tingled where they'd brushed his shirt a second ago.

Candy cleared her throat—too fast, too loud. "There," she said, her voice quieter than before, betraying a softness she hadn't meant to show. "Try again."

Lincoln didn't move immediately.

There was a flicker across his face—something unreadable. Something still unspoken. Then, slowly, he reached for the cupcake, his hand grazing the table beside hers.

Not quite touching.

Almost.

And for one suspended second, she wondered—if she moved, even half an inch—would he meet her halfway?

She wasn't sure she trusted herself to find out.

Lincoln blinked, exhaled slowly, then refocused on the cupcake. This time, the swirl came out cleaner, more balanced. Not perfect, but definitely an improvement.

Candy stepped back, ignoring the warmth creeping up her neck. "Not bad. I'd give it a solid B-minus."

"That feels undeserved."

She smirked. "You're right. C-plus."

Before he could complain, a gentle chime announced the bakery door opening. Candy looked up, and a familiar voice echoed through the space.

"Oh, honey, I know I'm early, but I just couldn't wait!" Mrs. Parker, one of Patty's Cakes' most loyal customers, bustled in, her eyes lighting up as she spotted the cake-in-progress.

She had been ordering her birthday cakes exclusively from Patty's Cakes for years, and this one—a delicate sliced almond and buttercream creation—had been specially requested for her granddaughter's engagement party.

Candy wiped her hands and smiled. "You're not too early at all, Mrs. Parker! I was just about to put the finishing touches on your cake." She gestured to where a few decorative piping bags and sugar flowers were arranged.

Mrs. Parker clasped her hands together. "Oh, sweetheart! This is *exactly* what I imagined! My Annabelle is going to be over the moon." Her wrinkled hands fluttered over her heart. "It's not just cake—it's art!"

Candy laughed, selecting a thin piping tip. "Well, it helps when the person placing the order has impeccable taste."

She glanced back at Lincoln and nodded. It was a tentative apology for the interruption, and, in a small way, an acknowledgment of the moment they'd just shared. Despite his rigid expectations and strict adherence to the rules, there was clearly some part of him that didn't mind getting a little messy.

While she wanted to explore that more, she first had to get Mrs. Parker her cake. Trying to interpret and decode Lincoln's binary thoughts would have to wait.

Chapter Seven

Lincoln

Lincoln, who had been quietly observing Candy's busy hands prepare the customer's cake, shifted his hips slightly. He wasn't looking at numbers. Or ledgers. Or profit margins. He was looking at her.

As she worked, her movements were precise, yet fluid, her hands steady as she piped delicate lace patterns onto the buttercream surface. There was no hesitation, no second-guessing—only confidence, creativity, and something else Lincoln hadn't fully understood until now.

Care.

This wasn't just about selling pastries for Candy. It wasn't about profit margins or costs. It was about people. She knew Mrs. Parker's stories. She created something that actually meant something to the people who came through those doors.

Lincoln swallowed, glancing around. The bakery *was* cluttered, yes. The finances *were* a mess, and yet, Mrs. Parker was glowing. It wasn't a terrible business model.

The woman reached out and clasped Candy's flour-covered hands with her warm, wrinkled ones. "I don't know what we'd do without you, dear." Her voice softened. "Your mama would be so proud of the way you've carried on."

Candy's smile faltered for half a second, but then she squeezed the woman's hands back, letting that emotion settle before blinking it away. "That's the goal," she said softly.

Something shifted in Lincoln's chest.

People talked about "fixing" failing businesses, about calculating risks and investments, but Patty's Cakes wasn't failing because of heart. It was failing despite its heart. And, when he looked back at the stunning, intricately designed cake in front of him, he had only one thought:

Maybe they really could win this contest.

As Mrs. Parker left with her cake, Candy turned back to Lincoln, leaning her elbows on the counter. "You're thinking too hard," she observed.

Lincoln looked at her, considered denying it. Then sighed. "You take this place seriously."

Candy shrugged, glancing around the bakery. "Of course, I do."

Something in Lincoln's shoulders loosened slightly. There was more here than he'd been giving Candy credit for.

Lincoln's pen hovered in midair, his eyes tracing every column on the supplier list with brutal precision. Beside him, the ledger splayed open—a bleak mosaic of numbers that kept spitting out the same conclusion.

Grain Street. Again.

He exhaled, the sound quiet but deliberate, gripping the papers in his hand tighter. It was the third discrepancy in under two weeks. Not just a mistake. Not a vendor error. This was calculated.

"Tell me I'm overreacting," Candy said. Her voice was low, but thin around the edges, stretched tight with something she didn't want to name yet. She hugged a clipboard to her chest as if it could buffer the inevitable.

"You're not," he said, eyes still on the paperwork.

"Tell me this is a simple mistake."

He looked up then, letting silence answer until he said it flatly, "It's not."

The words landed between them like a dropped weight. The hum of the refrigerator and the distant clink of metal cooling racks did nothing to soften the stretch of air suddenly gone too still.

"That's another screwed-up supply order," she said, her voice hollowing out. "And from Grain Street Baking Co...again."

She was trying to sound level, but Lincoln caught the tremble in the last word.

He closed the file with too much care. Candy was standing too still. People didn't stand like that unless they already knew the truth and were desperately hoping someone would give them a softer story.

"That's not a coincidence."

She didn't flinch, but her whole frame tensed—subtle shifts

in muscle and breath. He'd seen it before in boardrooms when CEOs realized the downturn they were ignoring was about to gut their quarter. Only this time, it wasn't spreadsheets or assets—this was personal.

"Grain Street started supplying us back when—"

He finished the thought for her, his voice like sandpaper. "Back when Bradley handled your orders."

She inhaled sharply, a sound she half-swallowed, but it was there. A fissure forming down her spine.

"You think he's still connected to them?" Her voice was steadier now, but edged with strain.

Lincoln lightly tapped the invoice against his palm. Once. Twice. "I think vendors don't repeatedly short deliveries unless someone has a reason to look the other way."

He didn't push her when she went silent. Not yet. Her silence wasn't avoidance; it was processing—a puzzle slowly revealing its final, cruel picture. She was going to have to say it herself. Admit it, and that would hurt.

"Candy," he said, tone low—not commanding, not coaxing.

She ran her hand through her hair, leaving streaks of flour along her temple. It created a faint white halo against her shiny curls. "I knew something was off," she said. Each word sounded strained. "I thought I was messing up. Missing details. I figured it was my fault."

Lincoln recognized that kind of guilt—heavy, misplaced, familiar, like someone trying to keep too many things from falling down.

"You are not the reason the books are a mess," he said.

Candy laughed, her sound cracking short and bitter. "Now you're lying to make me feel better."

He met her eyes then, and for once, she didn't look away.

"Trusting the wrong person isn't a business failing."

"It sure as *hell* is."

Lincoln's grip on the pen tightened until the plastic bent. Shame didn't belong to her. Not for this. Mistaking a mask for a partner wasn't stupid—just human, and maybe he recognized that more than he cared to admit.

He peeled himself away from the counter—leaned against the prep table behind him as if anchoring one part of his body might keep the rest from going too far.

"Do you trust me?"

She blinked. It threw her off. Like he'd spoken in another language.

"What?"

"Do you trust me?" he repeated, calm but firm.

It wasn't a moment for comfort—it was clarity. He didn't want a yes just to make her feel better. He needed to know if she believed, deep down, that she didn't have to claw her way out of this alone.

She hesitated.

Then nodded.

Not big. Not showy, but it was enough.

"Then we fix it," he said, voice low.

Something shifted. An almost imperceptible bracing in her posture—new drive settling into her spine.

"I need to talk to him."

A muscle twitched just beneath Lincoln's eye. "Bradley?"

She nodded.

"What are you planning to say?"

"I don't know," she admitted, and her arms wrapped tighter around the clipboard. "I want him to tell me. I want him to admit what he did. Hell, what he's still doing."

Lincoln's expression sharpened. She said it as if the answer would bring closure. Like the truth hadn't already shouted itself in ledger mistakes and stolen deliveries. And yet—he saw the part of her still hoping for decency from someone who didn't deserve it.

"You think people who sabotage small businesses come clean when cornered?"

Her fists tightened at her sides.

"So what?" she snapped, pain seeping from beneath the heat. "I'm supposed to just let him get away with screwing over my mother's legacy?"

Her voice cracked, and he realized it wasn't anger. It was hurt.

Lincoln inhaled slowly, a tightness in his chest catching him off guard. The sudden surge of protectiveness. The quiet, burning desire to fix this—not for business reputation, not for balancing the books—but for her.

"No," he said, softer now. "But if you're going to confront him, you need a plan."

She seemed to hold herself steady with a firm chin and squared shoulders, but her breathing told a different story—short and shallow.

"I don't have a plan." It wasn't defeat. Not quite. "But I have to say something."

He nodded. That, at least, he understood. Sometimes the mind didn't need a strategy. It only needed release, and if she was going to step into that fire? He wasn't letting her walk alone.

Wordless, Lincoln reached for his jacket.

"Wait...what? You're coming?" she asked.

He slid his arm into the sleeve. Gave her a look—not smug, not challenging. Certain. "You think I'm going to let you confront him alone?"

Something in her relaxed. A little. Then she tensed again, the way she always did when someone tested the boundaries she'd built around herself.

"I can handle Bradley."

"I have no doubt." He clipped the words sharper than he meant, but no less honest. "That doesn't mean you should."

Candy's jaw twitched—halfway to an argument—when the back kitchen door swung open.

Bailey entered mid-cookie, eyes practically sparkling. She clocked the tension immediately, then turned her attention to Lincoln with dangerous delight.

"I'm sorry, were you guys just heading out?"

Lincoln nodded, "Yeah, we have someone to talk to."

Candy groaned. "Bradley."

Tossing her cookie in the trash, Bailey grimaced. "*The* Bradley?"

"Not now, Bailey," Candy said, grabbing her coat and Lincoln's hand to pull him away from her friend. She realized she was holding onto him and dropped it just as quickly.

"Well, would you look at this?" she crowed. "A reluctant knight in shining business attire."

Lincoln didn't rise to it. "Bailey."

She shrugged, way too pleased with herself. "I'm just saying."

Candy flailed a hand. "Can we focus?"

"Oh, I'm very focused," Bailey replied, practically purring. "It's just not on whatever you want it to be."

Lincoln turned to Candy, ignoring the peanut-gallery commentary as he smoothed the fold of his collar. "Where's he working these days?"

Candy hesitated. "Café on Mulberry. I guess he's managing there, now."

Lincoln nodded once. "Good. Let's go have a chat."

"Just a chat, right?"

He didn't answer. He didn't need to.

From the corner, Bailey cackled. "That's what I thought."

Lincoln had already moved toward the door, running through contingency paths in his head—how to de-escalate, when to step in, whether Bradley was the type to bluff or spin out.

Conflict wasn't his comfort zone, but letting her enter a room with Bradley alone felt heavier than any formula or forecast ever had.

Maybe this wasn't a rational decision, but it didn't matter. Right now?

It was the only one that made sense.

Chapter Eight

Candy

The door to The Mulberry Café swung shut behind Candy, trapping her in the sterile, modern environment of Bradley's new place. The space was polished...too polished...as if it was trying too hard to be sleek and impersonal. It lacked the warm touches that made her café feel like home. Here, customers could expect shiny floors, perfectly arranged pastries behind glass, and overpriced espresso.

It was nothing like Patty's Cakes.

Lincoln moved beside her, a steady presence. He didn't speak, and he didn't need to. His intense silence was enough to be intimidating. It allowed her to face Bradley, but she knew he was prepared to jump in if she needed help.

Bradley stood behind the counter, sleeves rolled up, with a smirk already on his face. A woman stood beside him, arms crossed over a pristine apron embroidered with The Mulberry Café logo. The crisp white fabric sharply contrasted with the deep blue of her uniform, demonstrating a polished professionalism that showed she took her job very seriously.

"Wow," Bradley drawled, his smirk widening as he looked her up and down, taking in the flour-dusted sweater and the tired eyes that no doubt came from putting in real work. "I never thought you'd have the guts to come here. What happened? Did you take a wrong turn on the way to irrelevance?"

Candy barely blinked, but her jaw tightened, and she slowed slightly, narrowing her eyes at the woman next to him as she wiped her hands on her apron. Candy had never seen her before.

Lincoln must have noticed the pause because he murmured just low enough for only Candy to hear, "Who's that?"

"No idea," Candy muttered back, barely moving her lips.

Bradley, of course, picked up on their confusion and wasted no time soaking in the moment. His smirk was slow, deliberate. "Oh, excuse me," he drawled, gesturing toward the woman at his side. "Let me introduce you."

He turned slightly, tilting his chin toward her in a way that felt possessive, or at least proprietary.

"This is Sabrina," he said smoothly. "She's been instrumental in getting The Mulberry Café off the ground."

Sabrina's sharp gaze swept over Candy and Lincoln, assessing—cool, measured, polite but distant. She offered a tight, professional smile. "A pleasure," she said simply, though her tone didn't suggest she was particularly pleased.

Candy looked around, glancing back to Bradley. *So, not just a barista then.*

Lincoln took a deliberate step forward, his steady presence beside her. "And what exactly is your role at the café?" His voice was casual, but Candy recognized the quiet weight behind the question.

Sabrina straightened slightly. "We're partners," she answered succinctly. "I manage the staff and kitchen, and Bradley handles business growth and supplier relations."

Candy's stomach dipped. *Supplier relations.*

Lincoln angled his head, his mind clearly working through the same realization.

Candy barely held back the urge to sneer. "How *lucky* for you."

Sabrina's sharp blue eyes flicked toward her, but if she sensed the edge in Candy's voice, she didn't say anything. Instead, she simply nodded politely. "Bradley didn't mention you'd be stopping by today."

"Oh, he wasn't aware. I'm here to get some clarity—there seem to be some discrepancies in Patty's Cakes' financial records."

Bradley's smirk flickered—just for a moment—before smoothing out. He let out a mock scoff. "Ah, always with the dramatics." Then, with an exaggerated flourish, he turned to the woman standing beside him.

She had been watching Candy and Lincoln with composed curiosity, but Candy caught the subtle shift in her posture—her arms tensed slightly, her polite smile thinning at the edges.

"Sabrina," Bradley said smoothly, placing a firm hand on her waist, his grip just a little too tight. "Meet Candy. I told you about her. She's the one I used to run a bakery with before I took things in a better direction."

Sabrina tensed up just a little, as if something seemed

off—but she quickly recovered. "Candy," she echoed, nodding politely. "Yes, you're—"

Bradley cut her off, smooth and smiling, tightening his grip on her waist. "She's the owner of that old place, Patty's Cakes." His voice was playful, but Candy heard exactly what he wanted her to hear beneath it.

Sabrina glanced at Bradley, a flicker of uncertainty and mild confusion in her eyes. "Wait, it was Patty's Cakes?" she asked, tilting her head slightly. "You didn't mention—"

Bradley's smile didn't waver. "I didn't think it was relevant."

Sabrina frowned, lips pressing together. "I mean, if she owned—"

"It's business," Bradley cut her off smoothly, waving a hand. "This is where we are now. No sense dwelling on the past, *right*?"

Candy's stomach twisted. He wasn't just lying about the details—he was *erasing* her.

Bradley turned back to Candy, his smirk dripping with condescension. "I have to admit," he mused, voice thick with faux politeness, "it's kind of poetic, you stopping by today. Seeing all this in motion. I was just telling Sabrina what a great opportunity this café has been for me, and, of course, how much work it took to get here."

Sabrina folded her arms, her expression unreadable. "Yes," she said smoothly. "Bradley says he couldn't have gotten here *without you*."

Candy inhaled slowly and steadily.

Oh.

She got it now.

This wasn't just business to Bradley. This was *personal*.

An ex-boyfriend parading his so-called *success* in front of her—his new café, his new business partner, his new *everything*—as if Candy were just another thing he had shed on his way to something better.

Candy's fingers curled into fists. "Cut the act. We need to talk."

Sabrina stepped forward before Bradley could reply, placing herself between them with a polite but firm smile. "I'm sorry—do you have a reason to be here? Because if you came here to cause a scene in another business, I'll have to ask you to leave."

Candy's jaw clenched. She knew how this appeared. She was the ex-girlfriend, showing up in the middle of a busy business. Employees moved around them with cautious looks, and a few customers at the tables were already watching the scene with quiet curiosity.

"Sabrina," Bradley interjected smoothly, squeezing her shoulder just enough to ensure she turned to face him. "It's fine. Candy's working through some lingering resentment."

Candy exhaled sharply through her nose. "Oh, you wish that's what this was."

Sabrina sighed, giving them both a tight-lipped smile, then turned toward Lincoln, who stood just behind Candy, ever-calm and unreadable. "And you are?" Her voice wasn't unfriendly per se, but there was an unmistakable edge to it.

Lincoln met her gaze without hesitation, adjusting the cuffs of his sleeves. "Lincoln Caldwell. My firm was brought in to assess the financial discrepancies at Patty's Cakes."

Sabrina blinked, glancing between Candy and Lincoln. The relaxed confidence in her stance flickered—just a little, but enough for Candy to notice. She turned to Bradley, clearly expecting him to explain.

Bradley didn't miss a beat. "Apparently, Candy's trying to, what? Imply that I stole from her special little bakery?"

Candy scoffed. "Little bakery? You mean the business that was clearly doing well enough for you to embezzle resources from?"

Sabrina's brows pinched together. "Wait. Stole? That's a pretty big accusation."

Lincoln stepped forward, sliding a neatly printed invoice across the counter, the paper crisp beneath his fingertips. "We've identified a pattern of unusual overcharges from Grain Street Baking Co., the supplier Bradley handled when he was involved with Patty's Cakes. You don't happen to use Grain Street to supply The Mulberry Café, do you?" He tapped the paper once. "These numbers don't lie."

Sabrina frowned, lifting the invoice, but before she could properly read it, Bradley let out an over-exaggerated laugh, shaking his head. "Wow. You really can't let this go, can you?"

Candy's patience snapped. "You...think I don't see what you're doing? That I don't know you've been sabotaging me from the second you walked out of Patty's Cakes?"

Sabrina's frown deepened. "Bradley?"

Bradley exhaled dramatically, rubbing the back of his neck as if this entire confrontation was an inconvenience. "Look, sweetheart, don't waste your time on this. Candy's just upset that she let her business get out of control." He glanced at Sabrina with what could only be called manufactured sympathy. "You know how hard it is to run a place like this. Some people just aren't built for it."

Sabrina's jaw tightened, her arms falling to her sides in a subtle, defensive posture.

Candy squeezed her fists so tight her nails pressed into her palms. He was playing her.

Lincoln, patient as ever, spoke before Candy could. "It's not a coincidence that Patty's Cakes has been experiencing repeated order shortages from suppliers that have conveniently never given your café issues," he said smoothly.

Bradley's lips tugged into a slow smirk. "It's called running a business."

Candy's blood simmered. "You mean—at my expense?"

Bradley shrugged, utterly unfazed. "I mean that if you didn't understand how things worked, that's not my fault."

Sabrina hesitated, her fingers still holding the invoice, but uncertainty crept into her sharp blue eyes.

Candy pressed forward. "Bradley, tell me something—why is it that every missing shipment I receive would be just enough to stock another café? Why have all your 'exclusive' recipes been eerily similar to mine?" She stepped closer, tilting her chin defiantly. "And why, when suppliers suddenly stopped extending my bakery credit, were you able to secure accounts under my old agreements?"

Sabrina's hands clenched around the paper.

Bradley's smirk persisted. "So paranoid," he mused, shaking his head. "And, desperate." Then his gaze flicked toward

Lincoln, assessing him with deliberate amusement. "And, I suppose this guy is your latest 'solution'?"

Lincoln gave him a once-over that was unimpressed before adjusting his tie. "I specialize in fixing disasters. And from where I'm standing," he glanced around the café, then back at Bradley, "you left a pretty big one behind."

The smirk *froze* at the edges.

Candy caught it.

Sabrina did too.

Bradley let out a forced laugh, turning back to Sabrina. "You see what I mean? This is *exactly* what I was telling you. She's threatened. She's jealous."

Sabrina hesitated, her lips parting slightly. And for a second, just a fraction of a moment, Candy saw it—a flicker of doubt.

"She does sound pretty desperate to blame you for her problems," Sabrina admitted, crossing her arms. But there was something in how she said it—a hesitation, a crack—just enough for Lincoln to catch it, too.

Candy exhaled, meeting Sabrina's gaze directly. "You think I came here because I'm jealous?" she asked, her voice steady but firm. "I came here because I thought maybe, just maybe, you deserved the truth before he does the same thing to you."

Sabrina stiffened.

Bradley laughed—but this time, it didn't reach his eyes. "Wow, are we really doing this? The 'woman supporting woman' speech now? Come on."

Candy ignored him, keeping her gaze locked on Sabrina's. "When was the last time you checked the books?" she asked plainly. "Really checked them?"

Sabrina's fingers twitched.

Bradley turned toward her sharply. "Don't tell me you're actually listening to this."

Silence.

Long.

Uncomfortable.

Then, Sabrina's head tilted ever so slightly. She met Bradley's gaze head-on, but her expression had shifted, become measured and calculated. She didn't say anything, but Bradley's mouth stiffened.

Candy's pulse picked up.

She had gotten to her.

Sabrina looked at the invoice once more.

Bradley saw it. His nostrils flared just slightly, but it was obvious. "I think this conversation's over," he said, his voice a little too casual.

Candy smiled sweetly. "Oh, Bradley."

His jaw clenched.

"You had your chance to be honest. We'll keep making calls and check in with Grain Street. Candy leaned in, whisper-soft, and said, "We're going to win Sweet Success, and you're going to look like a fool. Then you'll wish this was all over."

And just like that, she turned on her heel and walked away.

Lincoln followed, his stride perfectly measured, as if he had never doubted her for a second.

As the door swung shut behind them, Candy cast a final glance through the glass. Sabrina was still standing there. Still holding the invoice. And Bradley? He didn't look so smug.

Her gaze flicked to Sabrina, taking in the cool professionalism in her stance, the way she said 'without you' like a calculated move. Not an admission, but a test.

Sabrina didn't actually know how much of this was Bradley's work and how much was hers. And that? That told Candy exactly what she wanted to know.

Bradley was smart enough not to surround himself with fools. Sabrina was here for a reason. Whether she had a full understanding of who she was backing? That was still up for debate.

As they stepped out onto the sidewalk, the cool air hit her skin, sharpening her thoughts.

Lincoln finally spoke. "She doesn't know."

Candy hummed. "Not everything."

"But she suspects something."

Candy let a slow, satisfied smile curl at the edges of her lips.

She had a feeling Sabrina wouldn't be backing Bradley forever.

Chapter Nine

Candy

When he suggested she join him on the drive to his parents' house—citing an excuse about multitasking and not wasting valuable contest-planning time—she agreed mostly out of curiosity.

When Candy imagined his childhood home, she'd pictured a house that screamed *orderly perfection*: crisp lines, minimal decor, and everything as precisely arranged as the man currently standing beside her.

Instead, she was greeted by the scent of lavender and buttery shortbread, a cluttered bookshelf leaning against pastel-colored walls near a sunlit bay window, and a whole gallery of awkward childhood photos smiling down at her from the entrance hall. Candy blinked. This was definitely not the sterile, museum-like neatness she'd imagined.

It felt warm and lived-in. Among the photos, a much younger Lincoln stood out, positioned front and center on the mantle. He was grinning, flour streaked across his cheeks, oversized glasses slipping down his nose, clutching a mixing bowl like it was his prized possession.

Candy blinked. Lincoln? Smiling? With flour on his shirt?

"What?" Lincoln asked, catching her stare as he shrugged out of his coat.

She grinned and lifted a hand toward the picture. "Is that *you*?"

His gaze flicked toward the frame, then back to her. "Absolutely not."

"You liar." Candy bit back a laugh. "Glasses?"

"Contacts." His brows furrowed. "Why do you sound so skeptical?"

"Because that's not the face of someone who reorganizes supply lists just for fun," she teased, crossing the room for a closer look. "You look...happy?"

"...I am capable of human emotion," Lincoln deadpanned.

"Really?" Candy's lips lifted in a half smile. "Which ones?"

Lincoln was saved from answering by the sound of soft footsteps approaching from the kitchen.

"I thought I heard voices," a warm female voice called. "Lincoln Grant, don't you dare step foot into my house without a hello!"

Candy turned in time to see an older woman—mid-sixties, silver curls pinned back, kind eyes—step into the living room, wiping her hands on a faded dish towel, and then she spotted Lincoln. Her whole face lit up, with the glow a mother reserves for any human she's raised from diapers to adulthood.

Lincoln exhaled in that long-suffering way only sons can manage, but there wasn't a trace of fight in it. "Hi, Mom," he said, as he pulled her into a hug.

She held on a second longer before pulling back and cupping his face like he was still ten years old, she said, "You need to call more."

"I call every Sunday."

"You call for exactly ten minutes." She narrowed her eyes before smiling indulgently and turning toward Candy. "And you must be the reason my son is allowing himself a break for once."

Candy grinned. "I'd like to take credit, but I think he was mostly worried about leaving me alone too long. He thinks I'll ruin his filing system, or something."

Evelyn's eyes sparkled. "Oh, I like you."

Lincoln groaned. "Two minutes, and you're already enabling her."

Evelyn waved him off, taking Candy's hands in hers. "And who's this?"

"She's a client, and...a friend," Lincoln answered carefully.

Candy blinked. "That's the most lukewarm introduction I've ever received."

Lincoln shot her a look. "Mom, please meet Candy." Lincoln looked at her, his eyes softening. "Candy, my mother, Evelyn."

His mom beamed. "Well, any friend of Lincoln's is welcome here! Especially one who has the courage to tease him."

Candy *liked* her. She *really* liked her.

Then Evelyn's expression brightened. "I hope you're hungry, sweetheart. I just pulled a fresh batch of lavender shortbread from the oven," she announced. "Come sit. Tell me what's new in my son's world."

Lincoln groaned. "You're not going to let me get out of a full conversation, are you?"

"You know better than to ask that," Mrs. Grant quipped, already retreating toward the kitchen.

Candy shook her head, following after her, while Lincoln sighed heavily and trailed behind them.

The kitchen was warm, filled with the smell of butter and fresh herbs drifting through the air. Candy took a deep breath, already captivated by the simple yet addictive aroma of the cookies cooling on the counter.

Mrs. Grant winked as she slid a plate toward her. "Go on, sweetheart. Try one."

Candy didn't have to be told twice. She picked up one of the delicate shortbread cookies and took a bite, her eyes fluttering shut instinctively.

Oh.

Oh, wow.

It was simple, buttery, melt-in-your-mouth goodness. But then...a subtle, unexpected floral note hit her tongue that was smooth and light, with just a faint whisper of complexity.

She opened her eyes, inhaling sharply. "The lavender...it's unexpected."

Mrs. Grant smiled. "Yes, dear. You like it?"

Candy took another bite, nodding slowly. "It's subtle, but it's there. It's wild."

Lincoln gave her a sideways glance. "Why do you sound like you just had a revelation?"

Candy ignored him, glancing back at his mother. "How

long have you been making these?"

Mrs. Grant chuckled fondly. "Oh, years and years. Lincoln's father thinks lavender in desserts is nonsense, but I always liked it."

Candy grinned. "He's wrong."

Something was sparking inside her now, something familiar—a flicker of connection between this moment and the countless afternoons spent baking with her mother. Candy didn't know exactly what was forming in the back of her mind, but there was something about this moment that felt familiar.

"I take it you like to bake as well?" Mrs. Grant asked knowingly.

Candy smiled softly. "I run my mother's bakery. Well...I'm working on it. Lincoln's helping me figure it out."

His mother's expression softened with understanding. "Carrying on a family business is a beautiful thing," she said. "Not always easy, but special nonetheless."

The words sank deep into Candy's bones. She needed to hear a mom say she was doing the right thing...and mean it.

Lincoln watched the exchange thoughtfully.

Then, footsteps sounded in the hallway, and another voice, deeper and gruffer, called out. "Lincoln? Is that you I hear being harassed in my kitchen?"

Lincoln groaned.

Candy straightened with curiosity as his father stepped into view—a tall man with graying at his temples, an air of sharpness about him, but beneath that was warmth. His calculating eyes flicked between them before settling on his son.

He gave a single nod. "Son."

Lincoln sighed. "Dad."

Candy barely contained a laugh. *Oh, so this is where Lincoln gets it.*

Mr. Grant turned his attention to her. "And you must be the reason my wife looks so pleased this evening."

"She's Candy," Lincoln supplied, before she could introduce herself.

Mr. Grant's brow quirked. "The same Candy whose bakery crisis you've been ranting about on the phone?"

Candy nearly choked on her cookie. "I'm sorry...ranting?"

"He means discussing," Lincoln corrected quickly, shooting his father a warning look.

"That's an overstatement."

Candy glanced between them, a slow grin forming.

"Robert. Call me Robert." His dad smirked.

Lincoln rubbed his temple. "Fantastic."

Evelyn smiled into her tea.

Evelyn reached for the butter dish, her bracelets jingling as she spread a generous dollop onto a warm dinner roll. "I don't know how I ever lived without you, Candy," she said with a dramatic sigh. "Anyone who can make my roast chicken actually taste like something deserves honorary family status."

Candy grinned, nudging the dish closer to her. "I didn't do much. Just added a little extra seasoning."

"Little?" Evelyn's eyes sparkled. "Darling, you turned it into something magical!"

Lincoln's father, Robert, let out a low chuckle, though he didn't quite look up from his plate. "You always did have a flair for dramatics, Eve."

Evelyn tsked, as she buttered another roll. "But who would bring the theatrics if not me?"

Candy stole a glance at Lincoln, who sat across from her, rolling his eyes in silent agreement with his father, though a faint trace of amusement played on his lips. It was subtle, but it was there.

It didn't take long for Candy to figure it out as she watched the two Grant men interact. She had thought Lincoln was an outsider in his own family—not because they were cold, but because he carried himself with such careful caution, always measured in his words. But the longer she sat at their table, the more it became clear.

Lincoln wasn't just quiet.

He was his father.

Pragmatic. Even-keeled. Logical to a fault.

But something was different. Robert glanced up at his wife, something warm beneath his gruff tone as she launched into another dramatic retelling of the time, he accidentally dropped all the cinnamon rolls on Christmas morning.

"You demanded I help you frost them," Robert grumbled, shaking his head. "In my defense, my hands were covered in icing."

"Oh, darling," Evelyn mused, stealing a bite of her roll. "Your hands were covered in love."

Robert sighed. "And sugar."

Candy covered her laugh with a sip of water.

But Lincoln?

Lincoln just stared at his father. Silent. Watching. Studying. Was he seeing something, too? He inhaled deeply, breaking his stare as if catching himself. His fingers drummed lightly on the edge of the table before he finally spoke.

"Garage is packed," he said, clearing his throat. "The movers shouldn't have trouble getting everything loaded tomorrow."

"That's good." Robert nodded, his approval silent but solid. "Thank you."

"And that old bookshelf in the corner?" Lincoln added. "You were right. It needed reinforcing. I tightened the brackets."

For a brief moment, just a flicker, Robert's lips twitched into something close to a smile before he smoothed it back down. "Nice work."

Candy looked between them, realization settling.

This was how they *spoke* to each other.

Not with grand declarations. Not with effusive words, but with actions. Subtle, steady.

Where Evelyn would fill a room with sunshine and laughter, Robert appeared to be the grounding force.

Candy's gaze drifted back to Lincoln, her breath catching slightly.

Oh.

Lincoln didn't just inherit his father's pragmatism. He had been modeling it his whole life. A quiet but tangible weight pressed into her chest. Because Robert, after a lifetime beside Evelyn, had learned how to bend. But, Lincoln still hadn't.

Candy swallowed, staring down at her own plate, watching as Evelyn gently reached for Robert's hand across the table and laced their fingers together without saying a word. Robert gave her hand a small squeeze—barely a twitch—but it was there.

Lincoln kept his eyes fixed on the silverware beside his plate, but his fingers, steady and controlled, tapped three consistent beats on the table before curling into a fist, as if he weren't quite sure what to do with what he had just seen.

She hoped, for his sake, that it wouldn't take him too long to figure it out.

Chapter Ten

Lincoln

"How," Lincoln asked, his voice impressively flat despite the rising pulse behind his ribs, "did we go from testing two ingredient variations to seven?"

He studied the lineup of cupcakes spread across Candy's counters like battlefield pieces. The neat rows gave the illusion of control, which it most certainly was not.

"Oh, chef, how did my steak get so buttery?" Candy wiped her hands down the front of her apron, somehow smearing more sugar than removing it. "Whoa, look at that. Did we accidentally have too much fun?"

She looked ridiculous—proud and completely unbothered. Ever since he'd taken her home, she's been teasing him relentlessly.

Now, this. She was completely diverting from their production plan. He had no idea how she managed amidst the chaos swirling around her, but somehow, it worked. Lincoln gave her a long, slow look. "This is chaos."

"This," she replied, with a flourish toward the disorganized rainbow army of baked goods, "is science."

He sighed, already dragging a sheet of tasting notes from the growing stack beside her flour canisters. The corners were curled, and someone—definitely her—had doodled hearts in the margins.

"You said you had a plan."

"I do! It's called a tasting menu."

"We don't have the budget for that."

"Sure, we do, we'll just sell the leftovers in the pastry case."

He exhaled sharply and gave up the argument, setting aside the need for order in favor of forward movement. "Fine," he murmured, reaching for the first cupcake. "Which one am I testing first?"

Candy slid a plate toward him, eyes bright with mischief.

The cake was simple. Familiar. Soft, with a thick spongy crust, and a reliable vanilla glaze.

He took a bite, chewing with deliberate focus. Flavors he anticipated: warm vanilla, buttery with a hint of almond. Nothing surprising.

"Balanced. Familiar."

"Safe," she agreed. "This is the classic patty cake recipe."

Lincoln nodded, setting it aside. "And the rest?"

She grinned. "They've got added pizzazz."

He reached for the second cake with the sort of measured skepticism that years of forecasting and accounting had drilled into his bones. "Pizzazz isn't a measurable factor in baking."

Still, he took the bite.

And then paused.

Chewed.

Paused again.

His brow creased as flavor bloomed slow and deliberate across his tongue—something warm-spiced and subtle. Not loud, and not sweet just for the sake of sweetness.

It clung to him in a way the first one hadn't.

He frowned slightly. "What did you do?"

Candy hid a smug expression behind her fingertips. "Oh, nothing much. Just...adjusted." She wiggled her fingers with a bit too much flourish.

He took another bite, slower this time, chasing the exact thing that made it hum differently in the back of his mouth. The sweetness was familiar, but gentler somehow. Earthier.

"You like it," she murmured.

Lincoln didn't answer. Not with words. He set the cake down carefully, rolling it in his fingers like the texture might offer an explanation.

Then, instinctively, he looked at her.

Candy clapped her hands together, victorious. "Success!"

Disoriented and still aching from something nameless, he gestured toward the cupcake. "What did you do?"

She smirked. "Oh, nothing much. Just...adjusted. Instead of just vanilla, I added a twist. Just a bit of cardamom in the batter—it gives it that tiny, 'wait-what-was-that' effect."

"Cardamom," he repeated, nodding slowly, grounding himself in the familiar. He took another bite. Let it sit on his tongue. The flavor mellowed but didn't fade. It clung.

And suddenly, his jaw wasn't working quite right because she was leaning in closer to him, elbows crossed on the counter, grinning like she'd just outsmarted the entire FDA.

"Explain," he said, his voice lower than he intended.

She leaned in too far.

Her fingers brushed the side of his mouth.

He froze.

The world went still. There was barely an inch between them—so narrow he could smell vanilla on her skin over the almond and cardamom lacing the air. Her fingers lingered just half a second too long, delicate against the corner of his lips, and his chest kicked once, hard and unexpected.

When her eyes met his, it was as if his logic circuits shorted out.

Then—dangerously—she leaned in.

Lincoln's gaze dropped, unthinking, directly to her mouth.

The kitchen lighting was poor—warm and casting shadows on her collarbone. He sighed and inhaled. She looked like sunlight. If he moved even half an inch, they'd touch.

But he caught himself. Blinking, he stepped back a fraction, reclaiming space that suddenly felt too small. Clearing his throat did nothing to loosen the tight knot beneath his ribs.

He forced his voice to cooperate. "It's unexpected."

Candy caught him watching. Studying.

She watched him closer, her tone soft enough to curl around his thoughts. "Tell me something. When was the last time you enjoyed baking?"

He blinked. "What?"

She tapped the spoon against the metal bowl and said softly, "The photo at your parents' place. The one where you're smiling."

"It's just a photo of when I was a kid." The picture had clearly been on the mantle for years, a flour-covered Lincoln tucked under an apron, grinning a mile wide like the world had handed him a pile of sugar and permission to eat it all.

"That kid?" she said gently. "He liked baking."

Lincoln followed her line of sight; his breath caught somewhere in his throat. He looked back at the table—at the smudged counters, mismatched spoons, hastily relabeled jars, and flour fingerprints left from who-knows-how-many trial runs. "I grew out of it."

It was true. Sort of. Or maybe...it had been practical to write it down.

Candy fixed her gaze on him, making him feel like she was studying him from the inside out.

"Or you told yourself you should."

Lincoln didn't answer.

Instead, he let her words sit. "You know," she said, dragging a finger through the frosting drip on the mixer cord, "not everything needs to be categorized and broken down into spreadsheets."

His lips parted, half-formed a quip, but he didn't say it. Because something in her tone carried too much honesty to just laugh it off. So, he said nothing and reached for another bite of the cake instead.

As he chewed, he stopped analyzing and let the sweetness fill his mouth.

Candy licked a bit of frosting off her fingers and grinned. "You don't have to measure joy, Lincoln. But if you really need a number, this one's easily a twelve."

He huffed out a breath. It might have been a laugh. Maybe. Candy beamed.

He didn't reach for his pen or mark that change on the spreadsheet. He didn't get up to log the ratio in her chaos-coded kitchen notebook. Right then, Lincoln took another bite of the cupcake and let himself enjoy it.

Chapter Eleven

Candy

"No, thank you. It's purple," Lincoln said, cringing as Candy handed him another spoonful of ube ice cream. He eyed the spoon skeptically, as if it contained a lethal dose of regret. "How did you talk me into this?"

She rolled her eyes and bumped her shoulder against him. "It's healthy, combines sweet and savory, and is a unique ingredient we could use for the recipe—if you'd stop acting like I'm trying to poison you."

Lincoln leaned back, folding his arms. "I don't trust desserts that look like they were engineered in a cartoon."

"Spoken like a man who thinks spreadsheets are sexy."

Candy took another scoop for herself and moaned dramatically. "Mmm. Tastes like victory—and antioxidants."

Lincoln gave her a sideways glance. "Victory tastes purple?"

"Or orange, or yellow, or pink!"

Ahead of them, the tents of Serenity's Saturday farmer's market gently rippled in the breeze, filling the park with color and life. Sunlight filtered through the small fabric streamers hanging overhead, and the bursts of wildflowers gathered in bouquets decorated the street posts.

Children darted between booths with caramel apples in sticky hands, while the smell of sizzling kettle corn and grilled sausage hung in the air. Laundromat-sponsored bunting fluttered off the hot dog stand, and a local bluegrass trio played under the gazebo.

Lincoln pointed across a few rows to a rainbow-colored tent towering above the crowd. Ribbons fluttered on each corner like it was meant to make children—and apparently him—irrationally happy. "I want a kabob."

"That's your compromise?" Candy asked, smirking. "Fleeing from purple into the arms of grilled meat?"

"I'm making bold, strategic choices."

"You're craving protein because you skipped breakfast again," she said, looping her arm through his. "And we're getting the kabob. But not before we try Ms. Sally's lavender lemonade popsicles."

Lincoln groaned but glanced down at where their arms were entwined. He adjusted her purse against his hip and let her lead him through the crowd. "Do all your recipes bait innocent hungry people with dessert and veer into mysterious 'health' food?"

Candy flashed him a grin. "Only the good ones."

"You're going to make me eat Tofu."

"Not today, though." She laughed and squeezed his arm a little tighter.

They navigated through busy stalls of fresh produce,

small-batch honey jars in deep amber, baskets of golden peaches and ripe tomatoes shining like treasure in the sun. Serenity's market was full of charm—every third table displayed hand-made goods; mason jars filled with goat's milk lotion, woven straw hats, homemade candles, pressed-flower bookmarks, and signs that read things like 'Live Laugh Loaf' and 'Whine or Wine.'

Candy picked up a tea towel embroidered with tiny cartoon pies dancing. "Your mother would love this!"

Lincoln peered over her shoulder. "Are those pies winking?"

"Yes. They're cheeky."

"I worry about you."

"But you are charmed."

He didn't deny it.

They paused to watch a woman in a flowing sundress turn pillowy dough over a fire-heated griddle, pressing it flat and flipping with a flourish. Next to her, her husband skewered peaches with fresh mozzarella drizzled in something sticky and sweet.

Lincoln glanced sideways. "Are those...peach skewers with cheese?"

Candy's face lit up. "You've never had grilled peaches with balsamic honey?"

"I don't think I've even imagined it."

Candy handed a few bills to the woman and passed one skewer to Lincoln. "Welcome to a world beyond beige food."

He looked dubious...and then took a bite.

His eyes flicked up. Paused.

"Well?"

He cleared his throat and offered a slow nod. "That…is annoyingly impressive."

Candy beamed. "See? Food can be full of surprises."

Just then, a familiar voice rang through the hum of conversation.

"Candy Brinley, you didn't tell me you'd be here today! Some friend you are…"

Candy turned instinctively. "Bailey!"

Her best friend appeared between booths, sunglasses perched atop her wild blonde curls, holding Rosie's hand in one of hers and a woven basket of jelly jars in the other. Taylor ambled behind her in a wide-brim straw hat and ankle boots that somehow looked stunning with her sundress, and Molly followed behind them—clearly pregnant and leisurely chewing on a fried pickle.

"Well," Bailey grinned. "You two look suspiciously like you're on a date."

"We're ingredient hunting." Lincoln, still chewing his grilled peach, didn't deny it fast enough.

Molly tilted her head. "Are we now acknowledging that you two are a thing, or shall we continue to live with the charade?"

Candy blinked, laughing nervously. "Lincoln's still trying to figure out if he wants to kiss me or strangle me."

Taylor smirked. "Girls leave them alone."

"But look," Candy added quickly, gesturing toward Lincoln as if he'd still have evidence somewhere on his person. "He ate the purple ice cream."

"Really?" Taylor arched her brow. "Was it at gunpoint, or

did she ease you in with pomegranate brownies first?"

"She did say purple foods have more antioxidants," Lincoln replied dryly.

Bailey laughed as Rosie let go of her hand to grab Candy's and drag her toward a booth selling pastel-colored soaps shaped like farm animals. The women followed and began eyeing lavender-infused bath salts and orange blossom body butters as Molly declared they needed one of everything...for retail therapy.

Lincoln quietly excused himself to the kabob vendor. Minutes later, Candy found him sitting beneath a shady oak, contentedly chewing grilled zucchini beside a blissed-out Rosie with a strawberry slushy mustache.

She walked Rosie back to her mom and then plopped down next to him, handing him a drink topped with a candied lemon curl and a sprig of mint.

"This market is aggressively charming," he said, sipping his drink.

"Takes no prisoners," she agreed, tipping her head back to let the breeze hit her face.

He angled to face her, his elbow brushing hers. "Is this what it's like every weekend here?"

"Pretty much. Sunshine, baby goats in bow ties, and lemonade that hides its alcohol content like a favorite aunt."

Lincoln's eyes scanned her as she smiled at the horizon.

He was, perhaps, a man still calculating risk. He was still peeling back layers, but sitting beside her, his tie grudgingly loosened and the lingering taste of violet ice cream still cooling his tongue, maybe...he saw what balance looked like. It wasn't perfect, but it was happy.

Candy turned slightly, drawn by the weight of his gaze. She caught him watching her. His gaze didn't flick away when she met it. It held.

"You're not nearly as immune to Serenity as you pretend," she said softly, her voice barely brushing the space between them.

"I may not be nearly as immune to you as I thought," he murmured.

"What was that?" Candy asked, uncertain of what she heard.

"Serenity may be growing on me." Lincoln's lips quirked, but his eyes didn't lose that searching quality. "Don't tell the winking pies."

She laughed, bumping his shoulder gently to mask the sudden shift in the air—the way something under her skin seemed to lean in, just the tiniest bit.

He didn't pull away.

The breeze stirred around them, catching in the curl of her hair and tugging the hem of her dress against her knees. His gaze dropped there for the briefest second, then lifted her arms to her face, resting on her lips.

"No more sample ingredients today?" he asked. But his voice came quieter this time. Rougher.

"Maybe not." She looked at him, a little longer than she should have. "What made you leave?"

Confusion flashed across his face. "Where? Here?"

"Yeah, Bailey said you went to High School here."

He shrugged. "The people who knew you when you were younger always think they know everything. What did she tell you?"

"Not much," Candy admitted with a little embarrassment.

"So, you admit to asking questions!"

She bumped her shoulder against his. "Whatever. You asked questions, too."

He waved her statement off and took a long pull of the minty lemonade. "Hmm, tasty."

"Don't change the subject."

"School, life, or adulting mostly."

"' Life' like a girl?"

"No, I haven't really had anything serious," Lincoln admitted quietly. "I mean, I've dated, loved, and lost, but I got caught up in work and school. Then, I was focused on building my business. The last girl I dated was for almost two years. She came over every Friday, rain or shine. Until she stopped going."

"Wow, that sounds...full of passion." She scrambled to fill the awkward space. "So, you like your schedules."

"Yes, and no. It worked," he said, then reached out to brush a ladybug off her shoulder. "But I'm coming to enjoy spontaneous, too."

Her smile faded into something smaller, more private, as her gaze tracked the movement of sunlight sliding off the backs of the market tents. The warmth of the day had settled between them, and yet...a very different heat hummed just beneath the surface.

She could feel him watching again. Close, too close.

"Maybe you just need that special something that makes a little bit of mess worth it."

"Like ube?"

"Keep it up, and I'll make you go back and try a porcini."

He laughed, "I can't imagine what else you might try and put in a cupcake."

"Life is about experimenting, but maybe we weren't supposed to find the 'it' ingredient today."

Her words sounded hollow as she said them—barely connected to her breath.

Lincoln nodded slowly. "Then what did we find?"

She turned toward him, sensing a shift when their eyes met. The breeze stirred soft cotton and hair between them, and the smell of grilled meats and warm peaches still lingered in the air.

Her heartbeat bumped sharply.

Candy leaned back just slightly, and the angle caused her gaze to drop to his mouth.

They were close—close enough for her knee to bump his, close enough that his breath mixed with hers, just once, while hinting at the question hanging in the air.

A beat hovered. Quiet. Uneven. If she shifted—just inches—they would close the space between them.

It was Lincoln who drew in a breath first.

"Okay," he said finally.

The pause clung to the edges of the word, as if gravity had nearly pulled something more out of him.

"I think we're pretty close to finding what we're looking for..."

Chapter Twelve

Candy

A buzz from Candy's phone rattled against the worn wooden surface of the prep table. She wiped her hands before glancing at the screen.

Unknown Number.

Her stomach flipped.

She swiped to answer. "Hello?"

"Is this Candice Malone?" The voice on the other end was clipped, yet professional.

"Yes?"

"This is Bianca Thornton from the Sweet Success competition board. I'm reaching out regarding your application."

Lincoln, who had been flipping through receipts again, stilled.

Candy straightened. "Of course! Is everything okay?"

There was the briefest pause. "There seems to be a complication."

Candy's pulse kicked up. "Complication?"

"We just received another entry claiming a recipe that looks identical to your Patty cake entry."

Candy's stomach plunged to the floor. "What do you mean, *another* entry?"

"This year, one of our contestants submitted an identical recipe version of your Patty cake as their signature dish...a Mulberry Butter Cake. Since entries require a unique creation, we need confirmation regarding ownership to proceed with your submission."

Candy's grip on the phone tightened. "But—that's my mother's recipe."

"I understand, Miss Malone. Do you have a written record clarifying its origin?"

A lump formed in Candy's throat. The original, handwritten patty cake recipe had been kept in one place: the old recipe book that used to sit in her mother's office. The same book that, before his departure, Bradley had "borrowed" to help organize inventory.

She squeezed her eyes shut, fury flashing through her chest. He took it. And now, he was going to use it against her. *The Mulberry Butter Cake was his.*

She forced herself to take a breath. "I'll get the documentation. Just—please don't take my submission out."

We're giving you until the end of the week to verify everything or to submit a new recipe. All recipes must be submitted at least one week before the event. If you have any materials confirming the provenance of your family's recipe, please send them to my office as soon as possible.

Candy barely mumbled a thank-you before the call disconnected.

She stood there, phone limp in her hand, trying to slow the sharp, panicked breaths escaping her chest.

Lincoln's voice was calm behind her. "What happened?"

She spun around, eyes blazing. "Bradley," she spat, her grip tightening. "He entered the contest with my mother's recipe, and it's totally my fault. I lost my temper and threatened him. Not only did he steal her recipe, he stole our idea to enter the contest."

Lincoln exhaled sharply, setting his notebook down in one slow, deliberate motion.

"He has a lot of nerve," she continued, pacing now, her pulse roaring in her ears. "This—this is beyond stealing. He took my family's recipe and put his name on it."

Lincoln's brows knitted together, his analytical mind working through possibilities. "Do you have a written copy of the recipe anywhere?"

Candy dug the heels of her palms into her eyes. "He has the notebook—the original. I thought it was misplaced when he left, but I never found it."

Lincoln's jaw tensed. "Of course, you didn't."

"He's already got a head start." Candy groaned and slammed her phone down. "He's probably refined it, modernized it, and what if he's using it to win?"

Lincoln's next words were slow, deliberate. "Then we need to rethink *our* approach."

Candy stopped mid-pace, eyes narrowing. "Meaning?"

"We make it better," Lincoln said, his voice steady. He stepped closer, his gaze fixed on hers. "You've already been experimenting with ways to refine the recipe. Now, we perfect it—make it something only you can create."

Candy inhaled slowly, the weight of betrayal still heavy, but as she met Lincoln's gaze, something changed. He wasn't just offering strategy—he was willing to help her and believe in her.

Her pulse steadying, she murmured, "We...only we can create. I won't let Bradley take this from me. My mother's recipe deserves more than that, and with you here, I'm not alone."

Lincoln gave a small, approving nod. "Then let's prove it belongs to you in the best way possible—by making it undeniably yours."

A warmth spread through Candy's chest, not just because of the plan forming in her mind, but from the quiet confidence in Lincoln's voice. She wasn't facing this alone.

This wasn't just about competition anymore.

This was about reclaiming her legacy.

And with Lincoln by her side, she *would*.

Chapter Thirteen

Lincoln

With precise, quick movements, Candy tugged at her apron strings while Lincoln watched. She wasn't just getting ready—she was bracing.

He held his clipboard at the ready, but its usual familiar weight didn't offer solutions or comfort. He'd never seen her like this, and he didn't know if he should help her or get out of the way.

Vanilla, nutmeg, and something sharper hung in the air. He could see that adrenaline, determination, and anger were held in check by her measured movements.

When she spoke, the words weren't meant for him, but for whatever rising tide she was keeping at bay.

"Alright. Time to work."

Lincoln adjusted his stance, sensing the tension in her shoulders. His thumb rested against the pen in the clipboard's binding. "Are you sure you want to start right now? You just got off that call. Maybe you should—"

The look she gave him cut straight through. Not wild—just sharp. Controlled, but not cold.

"Should what, sulk? No, we start now!"

"Noted," he muttered under his breath. Logical argument? *Rejected.* Emotional combustion? *Initiated and acknowledged.*

Now, he watched her even more closely—beneath the glare and grit, he saw it. Focus. She wasn't being reckless. She wasn't spiraling. She was digging in.

Clearing his throat, he dropped the clipboard onto the counter and uncapped the pen. "Okay. Walk me through it. How do we make this cake better?"

Her energy shifted—barely—but the temperature of the room changed with it. "We don't just change it. We refine it and perfect it."

Lincoln tucked that word away. Refine. Intentional. Measurable. The kind of concept he could work with, as long as they both agreed on the same definitions.

"You said your mother wanted to enter this contest," he said, pen hovering.

She nodded, jaw tight.

"Then if she was going to compete, she would've made adjustments. What would she have done differently?"

For a moment, Candy didn't answer. Then her eyes traced something invisible behind the racks and clutter—some memory he wasn't privy to, but one he watched land across her features like shadow.

"She always said a cake wasn't just about taste—it was about heart."

He looked at her. Blinking once, brows drawing together.

"Heart," he said, and raised his pen to take notes, but felt weird writing it down.

Her gaze snapped back to him. That familiar arch of hers lifted, annoyed but teasing. "Yes, Mr. Everything-Is-A-Formula." She rolled her eyes—too practiced not to mean something. "Food isn't just flavors. It's emotions and connections between people. It's nostalgia."

He felt the rebuttal catch in his throat instinctively, but he didn't release it. Maybe because she might actually murder him, or maybe because he knew she wasn't wrong. Not about this. He'd seen it too many times inside these walls: the way customers lingered long after they'd finished their dessert, the handmade notes she scribbled on invoices, or the photos tacked above the front register. Sentiment wasn't efficient...or measurable. But here? It worked.

"So, we focus on nostalgia and elevation."

"Exactly."

He let the pen tip tap one corner of the clipboard in rhythm as he scrawled: *Nostalgia = emotional resonance. Need a wild variable = unique. AND NOT GROSS.*

He glanced back up. "What adjustments are we considering?"

She hesitated for just a moment, her eyes locked on the honey jar on the shelf. "We need a deeper warmth to balance the palate..."

He could already guess the answer. "That means?"

She reached for a small jar filled with golden liquid. "Honey."

Another scribble. "Instead of sugar?"

"Half sugar, half honey." Her expression sharpened, voice steady as she held up the jar, so it caught the overhead light. "It'll give it a richer sweetness."

He filed the term away—richer being subjective but worth exploring. He nodded, accepting the note.

"Anything else?"

Candy moved in front of the spice rack, her fingertips brushing over each label with quiet intent. Then her hand paused.

Lincoln felt that pause, and his pen stilled.

She reached forward slowly—more gently than he expected—and lifted the small tin of lavender.

"Lavender," she said softly. It was almost as if the word surprised her on its way out.

He tracked the motion and felt his heart tighten against his ribs. "Like my mother's cookies?"

"Yes." She turned toward him, a bit more fire in her eyes now. Not defensive—alive. "It's unexpected, but light and can be used to carefully add depth."

He knew what she meant. Just a little bit. "And what does it pair with?"

"Subtle citrus. Lemon, maybe. Or deeper...vanilla bean."

She was calm now. He could sense her settling into a rhythm. She wasn't just rattling off ingredients—she was creating something. Building it, balancing it with instinct. She was making something that was hers.

"Logical. Clean flavor profiles. Balanced." He nodded once. "We test it." Her grin widened.

He hated how much he liked seeing her look that way.

"That's the spirit."

She turned to grab the flour bag at the same moment he reached for it.

Their hands collided. Warm. Certain.

Her fingers didn't flinch. They lingered—resting against his, her skin soft and lightly dusted with sugar. His pulse stuttered under her touch, a beat out of sync. It was traitorous how quickly her presence threw him off balance.

Candy's breath hitched—he heard it faintly over the low hum of the overhead light. Her scent curled between them—vanilla, lemon, and something beneath it all...it was the lavender, barely there but unmistakable.

He didn't move.

She looked up.

Her eyes locked on his—no teasing spark, no challenge—just clarity, and something pulling her to him.

She didn't search his face. She didn't have to. The air pulsing between them was fragile now, stretched taut.

Lincoln didn't calculate the distance. He didn't remind himself why this was a mistake. He just leaned in.

Her breath met his, and their lips brushed—soft, uncertain—but it paused everything. It was hesitant, like the moment before a word is spoken. Gentle angles and still hands, as if both of them waited for the other to decide whether to finish what had begun.

He paused—and she responded by closing the small gap. Their second kiss was more confident. A sign of certainty. Not hurried. It was slow and full of longing.

When they parted, her gaze flicked across his mouth, a hint

of a smile curling at her lips.

She cleared her throat—gently, the moment still clinging to her voice. "We need good numbers."

He swallowed, the corner of his mouth twitching as her hand slipped away.

"We need consistency in the measurements," he replied, even though his balance hadn't returned.

The absence of her skin against his was a void—small, but immediate. She turned back to the counter, reclaiming motion with steadier hands. He mirrored her, pen back in grip, clipboard grounding him in something familiar, but the room was no longer the same.

Between flour and honey, cinnamon and silence, something had shifted.

They worked now with a different rhythm—lavender folded into the batter, lemon zest covering the table as it rained down from the planer, and her shoulder brushing his arm. Measurements passed between them without words. Timing adjusted through shared glances.

Each step deliberate. Each small touch electric.

There wasn't a number he could write down on his paper that would account for what had changed between them.

Two kisses. Five minutes. A hundred heartbeats, and all he wanted was a hundred more.

He wanted to feel Candy's pulse in her throat as she tilted the bowl toward him, and he observed the quiet tremor that still lingered beneath her skin.

Lincoln wanted to remember every detail, because he knew that the moment they shared had changed everything...for both of them.

Chapter Fourteen

Candy

Before stepping back to admire her handiwork, Candy piped a final swirl of frosting. Rosie's birthday cake was almost perfect. Pastel pink roses, curled around the edges, cascaded over the white cake. Violet buttercream swirls accented each flower, making the cake look like it belonged in a storybook.

Almost.

Because instead of focusing on the piping details, her thoughts kept drifting back to Lincoln. To the way his hands had brushed against hers in the test kitchen, and the way his eyes had lingered just a second too long. To that inexplicable, charged pause—where she'd leaned in to kiss him, and now was aching for more.

A splatter of pink frosting landed right on her cheek, startling her out of her thoughts.

Rosie, who had been holding the piping bag with enthusiasm but barely any control, gasped. "Oops."

Bailey shot Candy a guilty smile. "Guess I should've warned

ya. This kid goes rogue with cake decorating." Candy wiped the icing from her cheek with the back of her hand, biting back a smile. "How could I forget?"

Rosie, unbothered by her own chaos, grinned brightly. "Mama said I get to decorate the whole bottom piece! The big one!"

Bailey, elbow-deep in a batch of colored frosting, smirked. "Sure did, baby, but only if you keep all the frosting on the cake and not your poor Aunt Candy's face."

Candy raised an eyebrow, playfully suspicious. "Was that actually the rule?"

"It is now." Bailey winked, nudging Rosie's little hand in a more controlled direction.

The three of them worked together, adding extra details to the cake. Rosie with her gleeful enthusiasm, Bailey with expert precision, and Candy...somewhere in between.

It felt warm. Familiar. Candy hadn't realized she'd been missing their time together until that exact moment.

Rosie piped a slightly lopsided swirl of frosting and beamed proudly at her work. "This is gonna be almost as pretty as Captain Rainbow Furry Sparkle Pants."

Candy blinked. "Captain, what? Oh."

Bailey pinched the bridge of her nose, suppressing a laugh. "You know, it's that dang goat."

"He's the best," Rosie announced proudly, licking some frosting off her thumb. "Jackson lets me feed him snackies."

Candy snorted. "Of course he does."

Rosie gasped suddenly, her small hands flying to her mouth. "Oh! Do you think Captain Furry Pants would like cake?"

Bailey gaped at her daughter. "Absolutely not."

"But..." Rosie's face scrunched in deep contemplation before she turned pleading eyes toward Candy. "Maybe just a tiny taste?"

Candy lifted her hands. "Oh no, kiddo. Don't drag me into this debate."

Rosie sighed dramatically, as if the weight of the world's injustices rested solely on her tiny nine-year-old shoulders. "Fine. I'll ask Mac later. He's nicer."

Bailey pointed a very stern spatula at her daughter. "Don't you dare get my husband involved in your goat bribery schemes."

Rosie, ever the chaos gremlin, giggled before backing away suspiciously. "Okaaayyy..."

Bailey narrowed her eyes, but Rosie only flashed an impish grin before skipping toward the living room. "I'm gonna go play now! But don't eat my cake without me!"

"I'm thinking about it!" Bailey called, waiting until her daughter had disappeared down the hall before exhaling in pure relief.

Candy laughed. "You know she's absolutely gonna ask Mac, right?"

"Oh, one hundred percent," Bailey groaned, scrubbing some rouge violet frosting from her sleeve. "And the worst part? He'll probably let her."

Candy smiled. "He was a catch. She's lucky to have an amazing stepdad." She smoothed out a stray swirl of frosting on the cake's border.

Bailey didn't miss the change in her expression. "He was and she is," Bailey said, setting down the piping bag. "So, now that my little distraction tornado is out of the room…"

Candy sighed loudly, already anticipating where this was going. "Bailey—"

"Nope, uh-uh," Bailey said as she hopped onto the counter, crossing one leg over the other like she was settling in for a long talk. "I've let you mope over this enough. Talk."

"I haven't been moping."

Bailey's look said otherwise.

Candy groaned, setting down her piping bag. "It's just…L incoln."

Bailey beamed. "Ah, yes. My favorite topic."

Candy huffed. "Can we not do this right now?"

Bailey folded her arms with a knowing smirk. "Oh no, sugar. We're definitely doing this. Spill."

Candy stared at the half-decorated cake, her fingers lightly drumming against the marble counter. "I don't know what happens next."

"You don't have to know," Bailey said softly. "You just need to want to figure it out."

Candy licked her lips, exhaling slowly. "It's just—it's been my mom and me for so long. Then me and the bakery. Then Bradley, and look how that turned out. I let the ball drop for a man. I've got to save Patty's Cakes. That's…that's all I've had to think about." She gestured vaguely. "There isn't room for anything else."

Bailey shrugged. "And now?"

Candy swallowed. "Now, I might want a *little* more."

Bailey grinned. "Took you long enough to admit it."

Candy sighed. "I just—I don't know what Lincoln wants. I know he wanted to help, God, I'm so lucky you sent him to me, but I don't know if he sees a future here. In Serenity...with me."

Bailey hopped off the counter, her smirk softening into something more understanding. "Sweet summer child," she murmured. "I saw the way he was looking at you at the market."

Candy's heart stuttered, but she bit her lip. "And?"

"And," Bailey emphasized, giving Candy's waist a light nudge, "He's falling hard. That man didn't look like he was planning on leaving anytime soon."

Candy's fingers stilled.

Bailey shrugged, casual but confident. "You just have to be brave enough to ask him what he wants next, too."

The simple truth of it was hard to argue, because she could ask him, but she didn't want to have to. "He left here once."

"He was young and starting his life."

"Yeah, a good one that's not here."

"People come home all the time." Bailey nodded to a photo of her and Mac on the refrigerator. "Or move things around to make an even better life somewhere else."

Candy looked at the photo and let her mind wander a bit. What would her life look like with Lincoln to wake up to every day? That soft pressure of his kiss, lightly flavored with powdered sugar, and someone who *actually* liked math.

"Hun?"

She jolted slightly, snapping out of her haze. "What? No. I was just—I needed a second. The frosting had to set."

Bailey narrowed her eyes. Then, her lips twitched into a smirk, and she shifted her hip. "Mmmhmm."

Candy grabbed a dish towel to distract herself. "Don't give me that look."

"What look?" Bailey batted her lashes innocently. "The delighted, completely smug one that says I know *exactly* why you're distracted?"

Candy groaned. "I'm not distracted."

Bailey took a sip of her iced coffee, watching her carefully over the rim. "You know, for someone who claims they're not distracted, you sure do sound awfully distracted."

Candy threw the dish towel at her head.

Bailey caught it, barely phased. "So. Lincoln. Are you going to talk to him?"

Candy's heart skipped a beat. "I might need to...we had a moment yesterday."

"A moment?" Bailey's smugness grew even more. "That explains the confused look and glow! Now, what kind of moment? Those can range from a light hand touch to 'I snuck out of his apartment in yesterday's clothes'? I mean, what woman wouldn't want to 'have a moment' with her very attractive, very level-headed business consultant?"

Candy sputtered. "It was just a kiss!"

"Oh god, that's even better!" Bailey grinned as if she had just won the lottery. "So, you almost went further."

Candy buried her burning face in her hands. "I hate you."

"No, you love me." Bailey strolled over to the cake stand, cocking her head as she admired the pink and pale purple piped edges. "Not as much as you secretly adore our dear Lincoln, but hey, I'll take silver."

Candy gave a half-laugh, shaking her head. "It's...it's not like that."

Bailey arched a brow. "It's *exactly* like that."

Candy groaned, pressing her hands to her face. "I don't have time for this."

"Mm-hmm." Bailey sipped her coffee, watching her carefully. "Tell me, did he look at you like you were his whole world before the moment broke, or was it more of a 'head over heels and totally confused by this' situation?"

Peeking between her fingers, Candy said, "Option two."

Bailey grinned victoriously. "Oh, hun, you are doomed."

Candy sighed, running her hand through her ponytail. "Bailey, even if I did—which I don't—I can't think about that right now. This contest is everything. If I mess this up, I lose the bakery. I lose the last piece of my mom's legacy."

"I wouldn't let that happen." Bailey's teasing expression softened. "And, you won't mess it up."

"You don't know that."

"You don't either." Bailey wrapped an arm around her shoulders. "But I *do* know you're doing everything you can, and, for the record..." She leaned in conspiratorially. "I've never seen you work this well with someone before. Not even with me."

Candy sighed, staring down at the counter. "That's what scares me."

Bailey frowned. "Why?"

"Because he's leaving." Candy swallowed, her stomach twisting at the thought. "He's temporary. This town, this ba kery...me. He's here to do a job, and then he's gone. He's off packing up his parents' house as we speak. That's why he's here, not because of me...not because of Patty's Cakes."

Bailey didn't argue. She didn't try to call her irrational. She simply exhaled and lightly bumped her shoulder against Candy's. "Then make it worth the time you have."

Candy's throat tightened. "And if it just makes his leaving harder?"

Bailey offered her a small, knowing smile. "That," she said softly, "sounds like a conversation for another day."

They stood there for a moment, the quiet buzz of the kitchen filling the space between them. Candy took a deep breath, centering herself.

She could focus on the contest. Think about a little girl's birthday cake. She'd save thinking about a clueless accountant with gentle hands and a wry smile for later.

Chapter Fifteen

Lincoln

Balancing the paper box under his arm, Lincoln held the door of Serenity Oaks open with his shoulder and nodded politely as a volunteer passed with a folded cart of towels. The air carried the faint scent of lemony disinfectant and something sweet, maybe applesauce or overripe peaches—but it wasn't unpleasant. The lobby was still and calmer than he expected.

He followed the soft shuffle of Candy's footsteps down the teal-trimmed hallway, his own shoes clicking against the linoleum. She walked with a careful purpose—neither fast nor slow—her posture a mix of practiced bravery and nerves she'd stopped trying to hide from him.

"I usually bring lemon tea cookies," she said, glancing over her shoulder at him. "But since we accidentally made four dozen of the lavender batch yesterday..."

He held up the box with a small nod. "Correction, we made forty-eight, we have thirty-four. You ate the rest for dinner."

"That's a bold accusation," she shot back, and though her

voice carried a teasing lilt, he saw the tension resting along her shoulders.

They reached the common area—a bright lounge decorated in shades of beige and blue, with sunlight pouring in through large windows. Two nurses arranged puzzle pieces at a table with a quiet older gentleman, and Mozart played softly from a nearby portable speaker. Most of the residents were older but alert, their expressions lighting up as Candy entered the room.

"Look who's here," one of the nurses—mid-fifties, sharp-eyed, with a bun so tight it probably hadn't been touched since sunrise—lifted her head and grinned. "Candy Brinley, carrying her world-famous cookies."

"Not cookies this time!" Candy's smile was gentle but genuine. "I brought my favorite CPA-turned-pastry-peddler to bring you guys a new treat today."

Lincoln stepped forward and offered the parchment-lined pastry box. "Lavender honey shortbread," he said.

"Well, I'll be," the nurse said, peeking inside before giving him a look of approval over her thick-framed glasses. "You must be the one helping her with Ms. Patty's old place. I hear it's been a lot of work!"

"That depends on the day."

Candy shot him a grin before turning toward a woman sitting in a patchwork lounge chair with floral armrests. Her hands were folded gently in her lap, and her eyes—soft and wistful—brightened the moment she saw Candy.

"Sugar," Patricia Brinley whispered.

Candy's smile wobbled, just a little, before she crouched at her mother's side, gently covering her fragile hands with her own. "Hi, Mama."

Lincoln lingered by the refreshments cart, unsure if he should give them space, but before he could decide, a new nurse approached him.

"You must be Candy's friend," she said, folding her arms. "I'm Ruth. One of Patty's nurses."

"It's nice to meet you," he said, straightening. "I'm Lincoln. Having her mother well taken care of is important to Candy. She talks a lot about how grateful she is for your help."

"Oh, I doubt that." She smirked. "Nobody tells stories about us old bats unless we're screwing up IVs or confiscating contraband fudge."

Lincoln's smile was brief but genuine. "It's the honest to God truth. She spoke very highly of the staff here."

Ruth's gaze shifted to where Candy knelt beside her mother. "Patty was the best baker I ever knew," she murmured. "I grew up in Serenity. First time I had a Patty cake, I was six. I had freckles, scraped knees, and an obsession with pink frosting. Her place was magical. She made every kid feel seen."

Lincoln glanced toward Candy's mother, whose lips were moving softly as Candy listened, nodding. "I didn't realize how much she meant to people here."

Ruth took a deep breath. "Seeing Patty admitted?" She shook her head. "Hardest day I ever worked. Because it wasn't as simple as a new client walking through that door. It was an entire history of birthday cakes, fundraiser pies, and Christmas cookie boxes. You'd never meet someone with so much sweetness in her soul."

Lincoln swallowed, something catching unexpectedly in

his throat. "She built something important," he said quietly.

"She loved Serenity," Ruth said. "Heart in every bite. Raised that daughter of hers to pour the same into that bakery too."

Lincoln's eyes flicked to Candy again. She'd made her mother laugh somehow—just a quiet bubble of joy in the otherwise still room—and he felt it like a ripple through his chest.

"I think she did give a lot of that to her daughter," he said. "She brings so much...energy into a room."

"Energy?" Ruth huffed a laugh. "She's an explosion of sweet chaos. Sharp, loud, messy. She doesn't have the peacefulness of her mother's temperament. Half the time, I think she'll explode from an emotional overload. You should have seen her as a kid. Ms. Patty had her hands full."

"Believe me, I've brushed up on 'duck and cover' and noted where all the exits are located," Lincoln smirked. "But, she feels big because she cares a lot."

But then she walks in here," Ruth said, softer now, "and the whole room shifts. Some of these folks don't remember what day it is. But they remember Candy. She smiles, and they do too. She brings light even on the days it's too hard to look for it.

Lincoln watched Candy with her mother. He was observing how everything functioned. In a room filled with almost strangers, she had turned every one of them into a friend.

She wasn't just fixing a bakery but preserving a part of the community that relied on her. And that had started with her mom. He could see how things he originally saw as flaws—her spontaneity, her insistence on following her heart, her rebellion against structure—maybe those weren't weaknesses.

It had been two days since their kiss. The kiss he was sure Candy had been pretending never happened because, well, 'business.' The woman was friends with everyone, ensuring her sunshine was everywhere. Notably, the one time she managed to be professional was with him.

But watching her, he couldn't help but think about the way her body had pressed against his or how warm she'd been. He wondered if she always tasted like sugar.

"Here they come," Ruth said, nudging his elbow. "They'll swarm you if you aren't careful."

"What? Oh."

Sure enough, a man in a green cardigan and fluffy blue slippers was eyeing the cookie box.

Lincoln brought it over, opening the lid and offering it first to the man, then moving through the circle of residents seated throughout the room. Each one politely accepted their little shortbread round, some with wide eyes, others with quiet reverence.

One resident murmured that it reminded them of their childhood. Another asked if Candy had really made it herself, and when Lincoln answered yes, the woman clapped like a child. By the time he got back to Ruth, she was smiling softly.

"Look at that," she said. "Now she's got you changing lives, too."

Lincoln's chest tightened. He looked back at Candy, but she wasn't paying attention to him. She was brushing hair away from her mother's brow, her expression soft and caring, as if a whole life was contained in that gentle gesture.

He had planned his world so carefully, and then she arrived.

Candy was messy, bright, and unstructured. None of his plans seemed to fit anymore. Instead of helping his parents and making plans to leave, he was trying to figure out what it would take to get her to kiss him again.

There wasn't a spreadsheet to help him figure that out. He could make a list of pros and cons, but he realized this wasn't an outcome that could be calculated.

But, helping her?

It was the best sort of chaos he'd ever known.

Chapter Sixteen

Candy

Either Lincoln was secretly a pinochle shark, or he'd learned the rules on the fly, because Old Man Louis already had him hooked for 'just one more hand.' She'd told herself that was ideal—Lincoln busy, happy, and distracted.

Candy leaned toward Ruth and murmured, "I'm going to make sure Mom is settled in her room. Can you keep an eye on him?" She tipped her head toward Lincoln, who was in the middle of dealing a new round.

Ruth's kind eyes warmed as she nodded. "Take your time, sweetheart. I'll see he's properly fed and adequately admired."

Candy's smile widened at that but faded as she turned toward the quiet hall past the common room. Her pace slowed the closer she got to the door labeled Patricia Brinley.

Candy took a deep breath as she reached the door. At that moment, the fear that her mother might forget her, that she might never realize Candy was trying to make everything right again, belonged only to them.

She turned the knob, took a deep breath, and pushed the door to open her mother's room.

The nurse had helped settle her mom by the window, her gaze distant as she looked out at the neatly maintained garden outside. The afternoon sunlight slanted across her pale skin, highlighting the silver streaks in her curls.

Candy hesitated for a moment, then cleared her throat softly. "Hey, Mama. I came to say goodbye."

Her mother turned slowly, as if she was reconnecting with the moment. Then, warmth returned to her expression. "Oh, okay, thank you for the shortbread!"

Relief pressed against Candy's ribs. Today was still a good day.

She walked over, settling into the chair beside her. "How are you feeling?"

Her mother took a moment, smoothing out the blanket draped over her lap before answering. "Good, I think."

Candy forced a small smile, but the weight felt heavier. She shouldn't have waited so long to visit. She shouldn't have let the bakery's problems take up so much space in her mind. Now, she needed answers, and if anyone could calm the storm inside her, it was her mother.

"I need your advice about Patty's Cakes."

Patricia brightened slightly. "The bakery."

Candy nodded. "There's a problem." Her words caught, but she forced them out. "Bradley...he took it, Mama. The Patty cake recipe. The real one and entered it in the Sweet Success competition."

Patricia's lips slightly parted as if she might say something, but her eyes drifted back to the window. Her thumb traced Candy's knuckle in a steady rhythm from somewhere distant. It offered comfort yet also caused hesitation.

Her mother frowned slightly, trying to focus on Candy. "Bradley…"

Candy's stomach twisted as she watched her mother's expression shift. Recognition flickered in her brown eyes—then faded, like a radio signal lost in the wind.

She swallowed to ease the tightening in her throat and tried to keep her voice gentle. "My ex, Mama. Remember? He helped at the bakery before he left. I think I trusted him. Too much," Candy said carefully.

A beat passed, long and soft, filled only by a breeze shifting through the half-open window behind them.

Her mother exhaled softly but didn't answer for a long moment. Finally, her hand rested over Candy's. "I always did trust too much."

Candy blinked rapidly, caught off guard. "Mama, this wasn't your fault."

Her mother's fingers traced slow, small circles over Candy's knuckles. "No. But maybe you knew, deep down. Didn't you?"

It wasn't an accusation. It was understanding. Candy swallowed hard. Had she? Had some part of her always known there was something wrong? That Bradley had been too involved, too insistent when taking control of the bakery's finances?

When she'd noticed things missing, inconsistencies, had she chosen to believe his reassurances because it was easier than confronting the truth?

Her throat tightened. "I have to fix it."

She pressed her lips together, but her voice still trembled. "I think I saw signs. I just...didn't want to believe it."

Patricia looked at her then, really looked.

"You're fixing it now?"

Candy nodded. "I'm trying."

Her mother gave another hum, as though she was stirring a memory somewhere inside a forgotten drawer and deciding it might still be useful if someone could just remember how to open it.

"Then you'll need the secret," she said.

Candy blinked. "The recipe?"

"No." Patricia gave a low chuckle. "No, maybe you've for gotten...sometimes I forget things..."

Candy sucked in a breath, glancing down at their inter-twined hands. Her mother's fingers had grown thinner in recent months, more fragile.

"Your Patty cake is special because you make it with love," her mother murmured. "That's what makes it yours."

Love.

That was...too simple. Too poetic to fight against something like deception and industry standards, but her mother's words floated in the air between them. There was no pre-made recipe for how to move forward.

Candy breathed in the faint scent of lavender that lingered on her mother's sleeves and shut her eyes briefly.

"I don't know if I can do it, Mama. Not the same way you would've."

Her mother gave her a small squeeze. Barely there.

"Then don't."

Candy opened her eyes.

Patricia smiled. "Do it your way."

Her breath broke. "But, what if I mess it up?"

Patricia's gaze softened. "Then you'll find a different way to make it better."

The knot in Candy's throat tightened. "How do you know?"

Her mother lifted a delicate finger and tapped it once against Candy's forehead. "Because you're my girl."

Patricia had built Patty's Cakes with joy, with *heart*. She had never been afraid to take risks, to pour all her love into what she baked.

Candy had spent so much time trying to preserve the past, trying to live up to her mother's memory, that maybe she had forgotten what made Patty's Cakes hers, now. What did *she* love?

Lincoln's voice echoed in her mind. You said your mother would have *made adjustments* if she were entering this contest. What would she have done differently?

Candy blinked rapidly, gathering herself before leaning forward and pressing a soft kiss to her mother's hand. "Rest, Mama," she whispered.

Patricia patted her hand one last time before settling deeper into her chair. As her mother nodded off, lashes fluttering like curtains drawn partway shut, Candy stayed, fingers still tangled with hers.

Her mother had built Patty's Cakes by adding everything she loved; now, Candy would need to do the same thing.

Chapter Seventeen

Candy

"Come on in," said Candy over her shoulder as she opened the door to her tiny apartment above Patty's Cakes, hesitating for just a second before stepping aside.

Lincoln followed her, his gaze sweeping over the lived-in space with books stacked haphazardly on a side table, a cozy loveseat near the bay window, and a framed photo of her and her mother sitting front and center on the mantle.

He'd never been up here before. Living above the bakery already felt like she was giving up enough privacy, so she guarded this place. Even Bailey didn't come up often. Candy gave pieces of herself away all day long to customers, to friends, and to the community. This little apartment was the one corner of the world that was only hers.

But tonight felt different. Something had shifted. On the drive back, she'd caught herself wishing the night wouldn't end, and she wasn't ready to let it. When she'd suggested grabbing some takeout, and that turned into heading upstairs, he hadn't teased her about how incredibly transparent she was being.

Lincoln cleared his throat and lifted the brown paper bag in his hands. "Where should I put this?"

"How about on the table?" Candy pointed to the corner where a small round table with a gingham tablecloth sat. "I'll grab utensils."

"Take out was a good idea," he said, setting the bag on the small dining table. "I've been wanting to try this place. Plus, it's nice to avoid making a mess we'll have to clean up later. I mean, if we're also going to be baking."

Candy scoffed. "Are you implying that I make a mess in the kitchen?"

He shot her a look. "I'm not wrong."

She opened her mouth to argue, but considering the pile of baking dishes in the sink downstairs that she would need to deal with later, she sighed. "Makes sense."

Lincoln smirked but didn't gloat. Instead, he unpacked the containers, handing her a carton and chopsticks. "Eat."

Candy blinked. Bossy.

She took a seat and started to twirl a strand of Lo Mein between her chopsticks, eyeing him. "So," she said, chewing, "what's your crisis meal?"

Lincoln arched an eyebrow. "My what?"

"You know, the takeout order you get when everything is falling apart, and you need food to repair your soul."

"There's no food that repairs a soul."

Candy gasped. "That is the saddest thing I've ever heard."

Lincoln hesitated, then exhaled as if she had worn herself out. "Fine. Dumplings, kung pao chicken, and, if it's been a really tough day, crab Rangoon."

"The deep-fried cheese pockets?"

Lincoln looked at his feet. "They're...functional."

Candy sucked in a breath. "Not everything has to be functional, Lincoln." She wiggled her chopsticks at him. "Sometimes it just has to hit right...which is why lo mein is the supreme choice."

He gave her a skeptical look. "Lo mein is the safe option."

"It has carbs. Salt. Sauce. Just enough soy to make you question your life choices." She shot him a pointed look. "It's perfect."

To her delight, Lincoln plucked a noodle from her container, chewing with sheer analysis. He swallowed, took a sip of water, then, after two long seconds, shrugged. "...acceptable."

Candy beamed. "Admit it."

Lincoln sighed. "It's not bad, but it's not Rangoon."

Candy laughed, nudging the carton toward him. "Maybe you just need more time to get used to the explosion of flavor."

Somewhere between empty takeout cartons and the kind of easy back-and-forth she hadn't realized she'd been missing, Candy found herself watching Lincoln.

Really watching him.

He was out of his usual buttoned-up space. His usual pinched expression smoothed out, and his shirt sleeves were rolled up, as if he actually intended to stay a while. Something about it made her stomach curl.

Lincoln caught her staring. "What?"

Candy stared at him a little longer.

Then, softly, she said, "Do you always work this hard not to let people take care of you?"

His jaw tightened slightly, but the reaction was almost imperceptible. "I could ask you the same thing."

Her stomach flipped. Because he wasn't wrong.

She set her chopsticks down and folded her arms on the table. "For your information, it's not a bad thing for a woman to be able to take care of herself."

"It's not." Lincoln exhaled. "But it's also not a bad thing to let people help you."

Candy stood up and said, "You're impossible."

His lips twitched.

Then, before she could talk herself out of it, she turned toward the kitchen counter and grabbed a mixing bowl. She felt Lincoln's gaze follow her movements.

"This is a very alarming way to change the subject," he mused.

"We're finishing the recipe," she said simply.

Lincoln blinked. "Right now?"

"Right now."

Within minutes, her tiny kitchen hummed with activity: flour dusted across countertops, spoons clinked against ceramic. They worked side by side, moving in harmony. He, with his practical, measured approach. She, relying on instinct and feel.

And instead of clashing? It seemed to work.

She reached for the lavender at the same time he did, and their fingers brushed. Something electric passed between them. When she glanced up, Lincoln was already staring.

There was a heartbeat where neither moved.

Then, before she could talk herself out of it, she reached up, brushing away a streak of flour from his temple.

Lincoln's breath caught.

His hand lingered at her wrist, holding her there for just a moment longer, and then he leaned in and kissed her.

It was soft, deliberate, and certain—like he'd replayed this moment a hundred times before finally letting himself have it.

Candy melted into him.

He wrapped one arm around her waist, pulling her close. The warmth of his touch spread through her, steady and sure. She sighed into the kiss, hands rising to rest on his shoulders, bracing herself as their laughter and nerves tangled together.

He broke the kiss first, just enough to meet her eyes.

"Maybe we've had the secret ingredient all along, huh?" he whispered, his voice roughened by emotion.

Candy managed a dazed smile. "Told you there's magic in the messy parts."

A flicker of a smile touched his lips before he kissed her again deeper, more confident, but still unhurried. The kiss was sweet and searching, full of all the things they hadn't said. Her hands bunched in the front of his shirt, pulling him closer, flour dusting the air between them.

They stumbled together, bumping gently into the edge of the dining room table. Lincoln steadied her with a laugh, his hands firm at her waist.

"Well," she teased between kisses, "so much for keeping the kitchen tidy."

He grinned against her lips. "Guess we're still testing the recipe."

Their laughter softened back into another kiss—longer this time, slower. It wasn't rushed or wild; it was warm and certain, tasting faintly of sugar and something sweeter still. His thumb brushed the corner of her mouth, and she caught his hand, holding it against her cheek.

"Candy," he murmured, his breath a whisper. "If you want me to stop—"

"I don't," she said, her voice soft but sure.

He nodded, eyes bright. "Chef's choice?"

Candy laughed softly, the sound catching somewhere between nerves and joy. "Baker's preference."

"I'm okay with that," he said, and before she could respond, he leaned in to whisper, "I happen to know you have excellent taste."

They kept kissing, laughing quietly, foreheads pressed together until the world outside the kitchen faded away.

The scent of sugar and cinnamon still lingered in the air, the oven's faint hum filling the silence around them. A light dusting of flour clung to Lincoln's sleeve and the edge of Candy's hair, and when she giggled, he brushed his thumb over her cheek, smudging a bit more by accident.

"Now look what you've done," she teased.

He grinned, eyes crinkling. "I'm improving the recipe."

"I think we've outdone ourselves already."

"Maybe," he said simply.

Her laughter softened. Their next kiss was slower—gentler—like the calm after a storm. It lingered, unhurried, full of something they both understood but didn't need to name. His hand found hers, fingers twining together in a way that felt like they had always belonged there.

When he finally pulled back, he stayed close, brushing his knuckles along her jaw. His breath warmed her skin. "Still good?" he asked, voice low but tender.

Candy nodded, her smile spreading warm and certain. "I think we just found a whole new secret ingredient."

Lincoln's grin turned boyish. "Guess we'll have to test it again...just to be sure."

"Quality control?" She asked, laughing softly.

"Exactly."

She leaned in, stealing one more kiss that tasted faintly of sugar and promises.

Chapter Eighteen

Candy

Candy stirred when she caught a whiff of something warm and buttery coming from the kitchen. For a few fuzzy seconds, she forgot she wasn't alone. Then, the faint clatter of dishes cut through the fog of sleep, and she was brought back to reality.

Lincoln.

Her apartment.

Last night.

She shot upright, sheets pooling around her waist. Her heart hammered in her chest—not from panic, but from the lingering heat of memories that had yet to fully untangle themselves.

He had kissed her, and she had kissed him back.

The whole thing had sent her balance spinning. Even now, her lips tingled at the memory of his slow, deliberate touch—at the way he had paused, just for a second, as if he was giving himself one last chance to rethink everything before throwing caution to the wind before they'd...well...thrown caution to the wind.

Candy took a steadying breath, ran her fingers through her hair, and slipped out of bed. Her phone glowed on the nightstand—6:23 a.m.

Of course, Lincoln was an early riser.

She took a breath to steady herself before sliding out of bed. She could do this. Be Casual. Normal. Not at all weird.

The memory of the night before flooded back to her in a rush of heat and want. It had started innocently enough, a current humming between them like something barely caged. He'd pleasured her until her thighs ached, until she'd ached and throbbed with a damp need.

Now, padding toward the kitchen with hesitant, bare feet. She braced herself for awkwardness, murky silences, and polite distances. But when she rounded the doorway, everything inside her faltered.

The loft was warm. Steam from the French press swirled into the air alongside ribbons of smoke curling off a pan. Lincoln was at the stove, sleeves rolled up, lean muscles flexing as he flipped pancakes with practiced ease. Soft light filtered over the counter. Browned butter and sugar filled the air, blending with a woodsy, clean scent—*him.*

Flour dusted his hip.

He looked so settled there that it was disarming.

She leaned against the door frame. "Smells good."

He didn't seem surprised. Just glanced over his shoulder, his eyes briefly skimming her bare legs before he looked away. He smirked. "Morning."

Candy moved closer, already noticing how thin her tank

top suddenly felt. "You made breakfast?"

"You had flour, butter, and exactly three eggs," he said, plating another pancake. "Pancakes were the safest option."

She watched him turn toward her. His forearms were dusted faintly with flour and streaked with batter. The buttons at his collarbone were undone—not enough to be scandalous. Just enough to make her mouth go completely dry.

"Well," she murmured, "normally people expect me to be the one making breakfast."

"I've had an excellent teacher. This seemed doable." Lincoln met her gaze as he set down a second plate. "I'm just making sure I don't ruin your kitchen before I go."

That word...*go.* It left panic spiraling under her ribs. "So, you are leaving?" The question escaped her before she could tuck it away.

He didn't answer immediately. He had just reached to pour the coffee, voice even. "Eventually."

The weight of it sank dull and heavy in her stomach. She'd known. Of course she'd known. She just hadn't expected it to hurt this way.

Feet moved before thought caught up. She wasn't sure what she meant to do—only that distance suddenly felt unbearable. Every step closer drew her deeper into the quiet hum between them, the air thick with coffee and flour and something she couldn't quite name.

She stopped just short of touching him. Close enough to feel the warmth radiating from his body, with the faint scent of cinnamon and soap clinging to his skin. "We'll need more than pancakes to make this okay," she said softly, surprising even herself with the words.

He looked at her—really looked—his gaze sweeping from her tousled hair to her bare feet, pausing at her eyes like he could read every unspoken thought. The moment stretched, fragile and full.

Then something in him shifted.

Lincoln dropped the spatula, the sound sharp in the quiet kitchen.

Before she could question it, his hand found her waist, firm and sure, drawing her close. Her breath caught as their eyes met, then his lips brushed hers in a kiss that was warm and steady, tasting faintly of coffee and courage.

The world tilted.

Her fingers found the counter for balance, brushing through a scatter of flour. On impulse, she pressed her flour-dusted palm flat to his chest, leaving a ghost of white on his shirt.

Lincoln stilled, eyes flicking down to where her hand rested. Then he smiled a slow, teasing smile that reached his eyes. "You're covered in flour."

She laughed, breathless and bright, nerves and happiness tangled together. "Occupational hazard."

His answering chuckle rumbled through his chest beneath her hand, and for a heartbeat, the kitchen—messy, sunlit, and smelling of batter—felt like the only place in the world that mattered.

He leaned in again, and this time the kiss was deeper, longer, full of everything they hadn't said. Her hands slid up to his shoulders, tracing the faint line of tension there. He responded by drawing her closer, their bodies fitting together in a way that felt effortless and familiar.

"You're trying to tempt me," he murmured against her cheek, his breath warm and teasing.

"I sell sugar for a living, it's sort of what I do," she whispered back, tugging lightly at his shirt, dusting him with more flour.

He chuckled, low and rough, and kissed her again. The world narrowed to the sound of their laughter and the soft scrape of the counter behind her. She could taste coffee and sugar on his lips.

They bumped into the counter, knees knocking, hips brushing as the bowl of pancake batter wobbled precariously.

Lincoln steadied her with one hand and kissed her with the other still resting at her waist, gentle but sure. "Careful," he murmured between kisses. "You'll ruin breakfast."

"Pretty sure breakfast's already ruined," she said, smiling against his lips.

Flour puffed into the air around them, settling over his hair and her bare arm. They both laughed. The sound filled the kitchen.

He pressed his forehead to hers, eyes soft and searching. "Candy..."

She lifted a hand, brushing her thumb along his jaw. "I know," she whispered. "I don't want to think about you leaving yet."

Lincoln's expression softened. "Then don't."

They stayed close, hands intertwined, breaths mingling in the small space between them. The scent of warm batter and coffee wrapped around them as if the entire morning had been made for just this.

After a while, he brushed a bit of flour from her nose and smiled. "We're a mess."

She grinned. "I like it that way."

He bent down, kissed her again—slower this time, lingering just enough to promise more without rushing it.

When they finally pulled apart, Candy rested her hands against his chest, smiling through the haze of flour and sunlight. "This was..."

"Necessary," Lincoln finished, his voice rough with warmth. "Desperately."

She laughed softly as he reached for a towel, brushing flour from her arm.

"Well," she said with a crooked smile, "so much for not making a mess in my kitchen."

Lincoln smirked, flicking a bit of flour her way. "Want a pancake?"

"Only if we can share it," she teased.

He grinned. "Deal."

And just like that, the kitchen filled with laughter again, two hearts beating in rhythm with the soft sizzle of batter on the stove and the promise that *this* morning wouldn't be their last together.

Chapter Nineteen

Candy

Leaning against the bakery counter, Candy stared down at the latest practice batch of their lavender-infused Patty cakes. "They're good," Lincoln admitted from his seat across from her, adjusting the glasses he'd worn instead of his contacts.

She was just a little fascinated by how the glasses gave him a Clark Kent air, and she was curious to explore that more, but before Candy could respond, the front door chimed.

"Please tell me you've got something sweet and life-changing coming out of that oven," a familiar voice called.

Candy turned just in time to see Taylor walking into the bakery. The owner of A Stitch in Time, Serenity's go-to clothing consignment shop, wore a bright purple scarf draped around her neck, her arms holding a neatly wrapped package. The woman had a talent for making an entrance, and today was no different.

"Taylor, what are you doing here?" asked Candy.

Taylor placed the package on the counter, giving Candy

a pointed look. "What? A girl can't stop by and support her favorite baker?"

Candy smirked, relaxing a fraction. "Usually when you 'stop by' unannounced, it means you have an ulterior motive."

Taylor gasped dramatically, placing a hand on her chest. "How dare you accuse me of such things?" Then, with an eye roll, she added, "Okay, fine, maybe I came to see the man Bailey keeps talking about, along with a small request."

"She needs to learn to stop talking." Candy threw a testing glance at Lincoln and folded her arms. "Go on."

Taylor smirked. "I'm hosting a customer appreciation event this weekend at the shop, and I'd love to have a little catered selection of your best sweets...something fancy, something indulgent. Think 'Parisian café meets Texas charm.'"

Candy's stomach twisted briefly. Her catering orders had been inconsistent lately, caught between bakery difficulties and Sweet Success preparations, but Taylor's warm smile eased her worries.

Taylor wanted to support her, not just as a friend, but as a client.

Candy exhaled, her lips curling into a grateful smile. "You got it. I'll put together something special."

Taylor clapped her hands together. "Fabulous." Then, her sharp gaze flicked to the tray of test cupcakes. "Now, what's this? A new Patty Cake recipe?"

"Bailey told you everything?" Candy shrugged and nodded. "We're trying to perfect a final contest variation on the original Patty Cake recipe. We've added lavender, but it's still missing something."

Taylor's brows lifted with interest. "Well, don't leave me out of the fun. Hand one over."

Candy grabbed a cupcake and placed it in front of her friend. Taylor peeled back the wrapper with the kind of reverence she usually reserved for vintage Chanel and designer handbags before taking a slow, measured bite.

Both Candy and Lincoln watched...waiting.

Taylor chewed thoughtfully, her expression unreadable. Then, finally, she swallowed and gave a small nod. "It's good."

Candy tilted her head. "'Good'?"

Taylor hesitated, then twisted her lips slightly. "It's really good. Like, I'd definitely buy another."

"But?" Lincoln pressed.

Taylor sighed, giving Candy a look. "But it's not the best I've ever had."

Candy's stomach flipped slightly. "What's missing?"

Taylor hummed thoughtfully, tapping a manicured nail on the countertop. "It's balanced, the flavors are airy and refined—but maybe too refined? It's delicate." She paused for a moment before snapping her fingers. "Maybe it needs a richer base flavor. Like vanilla bean or browned butter instead of regular." She waved a hand. "Something that lingers."

Candy blinked, processing. *Browned butter.*

She turned slightly toward Lincoln, who had pulled out his clipboard again, jotting something down. He inclined his head toward her.

"It's a strong note," he admitted. "Could give it the depth it needs."

Candy nodded slowly. "Browned butter would add richness and keep the floral notes from overpowering it."

Taylor grinned. "See? That's why I shop and snack at the same time—maximum inspiration."

Candy shook her head and laughed as Taylor pointed to the unopened package she had brought.

"Speaking of inspiration," she added, nudging it forward, "I found this at the shop and thought of you."

Curious, Candy peeled back the tissue paper, revealing a vintage apron in delicate cream with floral accents, the stitching intricate and worn in the best way.

Candy's throat clenched. "Taylor…"

Taylor shrugged, looking unexpectedly shy. "I figured you could use some extra luck for the big day."

Candy ran her hand over the fabric. It reminded her of something her mother would've worn once upon a time. Warm. Nostalgic. Like home.

A small, genuine smile curled across her lips. "I love it."

Taylor beamed, brushing off imaginary dust from her shoulder. "Good. Now, I'll leave you, culinary geniuses, to your fine-tuning. Just make sure I get my catering order *before* you become famous!"

With a wink, she grabbed her purse and headed for the door, calling over her shoulder, "Oh, and whatever you add to that new Patty Cake? It's going to be the best thing there."

The door chimed as she left, leaving Candy staring after her.

Lincoln watched. "You really have the entire town rooting for you."

Candy exhaled, turning back toward the tray of cakes. "Now, I just have to make sure I don't let them down."

Lincoln nodded. "Let's figure out what it's missing."

He didn't need to say it, but the message was obvious. They'd figure it out together. And just in time, because as Taylor's car disappeared down the road, the door chimed again.

Candy looked up and immediately went stiff.

Bradley.

The easy atmosphere hardened instantly.

He strode in like he owned the place, his walk casual yet deliberate. The smug tilt of his lips sent a familiar, unwelcome spark of fury through her.

Lincoln didn't move, but she *felt* him shift, his presence solidifying like stone.

"Wow," Bradley drawled, eyes flicking across the quiet bakery. "Slow day, I see. Where's the usual morning rush?"

Candy folded her arms. "What do you want, Bradley?"

His smirk widened. "Now, is that any way to greet an old friend?"

"You're not my friend."

Bradley sighed dramatically, placing a hand over his chest. "So cold. Harsh words from someone who once trusted me with her entire bakery."

Lincoln's chair scraped softly against the floor as he sat upright.

Bradley's smirk grew sharper as he casually checked Lincoln out. "And look—someone is still in town. Sticking around for the free pastries? Or is she handing out samples of something else?"

Lincoln remained perfectly unbothered. "You're deflecting."

Bradley's eyes flickered with something unreadable before shifting back to Candy. "Fine. Let's cut to it. I came to check in before we face off at Sweet Success."

Candy narrowed her eyes. "Why?"

He sighed as if he was tired of explaining things to her. "Because I'm being considerate, Candy."

Lincoln exhaled, unimpressed. "You? Considerate."

Bradley ignored him, keeping his voice deceptively smooth. "I just think the competition might be...a bit much for you right now."

Candy stilled.

Bradley pretended to look around the kitchen with mild disinterest. "I mean, really. Between your struggling bakery and your mom's condition—"

Lincoln's chair scraped back.

Bradley barely flinched, but she noticed how his fingers twitched once at his side.

Lincoln's voice was calm. Too calm. "Tread carefully."

Bradley let out a sharp breath before lazily rolling his shoulders. "Relax, I'm just saying...taking on this contest might not be the best idea. Maybe you should step down, and avoid the humiliation of losing."

Candy went very, very still.

Lincoln observed it—the slack in her shoulders, the tightness in her jaw.

Bradley smirked. "Think about it, Candy. If you back out now, you can avoid all that bad publicity. It's a win-win."

For a brief moment, she finally saw it...him, really...with perfect clarity.

The way he always spoke down to her, the way he *allowed* her to make decisions about her own business, and the way he made her doubt herself so completely that she didn't even notice him stealing from her until it was too late.

Bradley still believed she was the same woman he had manipulated and controlled. He assumed she would back down.

When it clicked into place, she stepped forward slowly, closing the gap between them. "Bradley," she said, voice dangerously sweet. "Let me make something excruciatingly clear."

He blinked.

She lifted her chin, eyes steady. "I would rather *burn Patty's Cakes to the ground* than let you take one more thing from me."

Bradley's smirk twitched.

Lincoln, silent but right there, didn't move, but she felt him noting every flicker of emotion passing over Bradley's smug face.

A slow nod, a sharp exhale through Bradley's nose, and then, with a mock casual air, he stepped back toward the door. "Fine. Have it your way," he said, slipping his hands into his pockets. Then, just as he reached for the handle, he looked over his shoulder with a lazy grin. "See you at the competition."

Then he was gone.

The second the door shut, Lincoln muttered something decidedly unprofessional under his breath and turned to her. "You okay?"

Candy inhaled deeply, grounding herself.

She felt the heat of anger burning in her bloodstream, but beneath it all was *resolve.*

She met Lincoln's gaze, fire in her eyes.

"No," she said, voice steady. "I'm ready."

Lincoln sat thinking, for a long moment, unreadable.

Then, after a beat, he smirked, a slow, deliberate curve of the lips that sent a thrill down her spine.

"Good."

Chapter Twenty

Lincoln

Dust clung to everything.

It lined the grooves of wooden shelves, dulled every cardboard crease, softened the faded marker that spelled "Donate" on boxes he'd packed without looking twice. Sunlight knifed through the garage windows in angled bars, highlighting the haze in the air.

Lincoln wiped the back of his wrist across his brow, the grit scratching at his skin, and leaned further into the open box in front of him. His back twinged, protesting, but it was easier to focus on the physical discomfort than the press of unspoken things building between them.

Candy had happily agreed to help his parents with the last of their garage cleanout. He had promised them a week ago that he would collect his things. Now, across the cluttered garage, Candy held up a worn baseball glove, the leather sun-softened and familiar in a way that tugged at something he didn't want to name.

"Keep or donate?" she asked.

His voice came without effort. "Donate."

There was a pause. "Wait—you're really getting rid of that?"

He looked up. She was staring at the glove like it had just whispered some memory into her hand. Brow knit, eyes questioning. He hadn't expected her to hesitate. Not over something like that, but he could tell working together like this was only reminding her what would come next...his departure.

"Haven't used it since high school," he said.

Candy carefully turned the glove over, tracing the faded ink stitched through the wrist strap. "But it's yours. Your name's literally written on it."

He held out his hand. When their fingers brushed, her skin was warm from sunlight and effort. She smelled of vanilla and sugar, a scent he recognized as *hers*.

When he took the glove, it felt smaller—light, broken in, too soft to grip anything firmly. Holding it triggered something that made his throat tighten. Not sorrow. Not nostalgia. Just recognition of a version of himself he'd packed away a long time ago. On purpose.

He dropped it into the pile.

Candy didn't miss a beat. She reached in and pulled it right back out, like she was rescuing something from oblivion.

Her voice lowered, but didn't lose its edge. "This isn't just some random thing. Look at it. It's broken in just right."

Lincoln pressed a thumb to the angle of his jaw, trying for control in motion. "And? It's not like I'm applying for spring training."

But even as the words left his mouth, he could hear the thinness in them.

She didn't let up. Her fingers moved over the curve of the glove as if she could feel the echoes it contained. She stepped closer, until she was close enough for her voice to sound softer than usual.

"This belonged to young Lincoln." Then, even softer, her hand grazing the stubble on his jaw, "Didn't he care about it?"

He should've shrugged and brushed it off, but instead, his body leaned — barely — a delay between his sense and reaction, just enough to give his truth away, and then she kissed him.

It was light. Sure. Warm enough to stir every carefully stored part of him. His arms moved before he could think, holding her tight and deepening the kiss in a way that felt almost too easy. She tasted like strawberry frosting and something wilder beneath.

She tasted like risk.

It settled into his chest, warm and heady, sparking in the space between his ribs.

He pulled back first, voice lower than he intended. "If we keep this up, nothing's getting done."

Her lips trembled. "Well, if you're just going to get rid of everything, we've got plenty of time." But her tone carried something sharper beneath the tease.

He didn't answer because it wasn't about time or clutter. Not really.

She gestured at the pile behind them, the half-sorted detritus of a boy-turned-man.

"You're just tossing all this out? No second thoughts?"

Lincoln straightened, folding his arms across his chest to cover the way tension crept under his skin. "It's just stuff."

It came out too fast. Even to his ears, it rang hollow.

Candy rose slowly; her movements were deliberate now. "Yeah?" she said. Her voice sharpened. "And what happens when you move on from Serenity? From—"

She clipped the word, but he heard it anyway.

Me caught and swallowed mid-sentence and was left hanging in the heat between them.

His stomach twisted into a tight knot, and she tried to backpedal, throwing out a joke to soften the edge, but the moment had already been broken. They might have been able to recover, but she followed it with something quieter. Meaner.

"You don't even hesitate before tossing things aside. Memories, moments—people. Everything's temporary, right?"

He blinked. The air inside the garage thinned.

That wasn't anger in her voice.

It was *loss*. He heard it when she talked about her mom, and now him.

"That's not..." The words crawled up his throat and stalled, dry and unconvincing.

He saw it now; she wasn't flaring like she usually did. Not combusting on emotion. She'd already burned through that. Now she was ashes and aches.

"It's not fair," he said, softer.

She let out a half-laugh, raw and dry where it broke. "Isn't it? People leave, Lincoln. That's just what they do." She turned away, with no drama in her motion, just inevitability. "You'd know all about that."

The hit landed with surgical precision—not because it was cruel, but because it was real.

He let the silence grow between them, thick as dust in the air. Watched how her shoulders curled inward, as if she was trying to vanish into herself. No apron, no jokes, no flour to distract from the hurt.

She was wound tight, like a cord with nowhere left to pull.

He picked up a box. It didn't matter what was inside.

Cracked vinyl albums, blank school records, maybe a dissolved version of who he used to be. He shoved past the tape and held it out.

"Can you put this in the car?"

She took it, wordlessly. Her fingers were steady, her grip efficient, but they brushed his again on the way out, and this time, the touch felt more like a goodbye.

He watched her walk out toward the garage's open door. The sun outside painted her in gold, but the line of her spine told him what she wouldn't say out loud.

She thought he threw things away because he didn't care, believing he simplified the aftermath of intimacy, making the discard seem effortless. He'd given her reasons to think that, and he hadn't exactly made it easy to believe otherwise.

But the problem wasn't that he didn't care—it was that he cared too much. Careful enough to disconnect first. Careful enough to walk away before he got left. He watched her form fade into shadow at the end of the driveway.

Then quietly, his hands pressed more tightly around the edges of the open box, the cardboard biting into his palms.

Because he'd let go of things in the past.

But this?

This wasn't something he just wasn't sure he was ready to lose.

Lincoln kept his eyes on the road, the dashboard casting faint orange light over his hands at ten and two. Outside, the dark Texas night slid past in silver seams of headlights and dissolving shadows. Inside the car, silence simmered, dense and tight as rising dough sealed too long under a bowl.

From the passenger seat, Candy shifted again, arms folded tightly to her body. Her foot tapped against the floorboards—nothing setting the rhythm. A coil of energy sat next to him, ready to explode.

"You're too quiet," she muttered, her voice cutting through the cabin like the sudden hush before a fire alarm.

Lincoln kept his jaw steady. "I wasn't aware there was a required amount of conversation."

Out of the corner of his eye, her shoulders tensed, a telltale sign of tension that made him brace for impact. "You know what I mean," she said.

And he did. He knew the exact pitch of that frustration, and the undertow she didn't want to name. It was something deeper than anger, older. Something he had earned.

His fingers flexed over the wheel. The coarse grain of the leather pressed against his palm.

"You picked a fight back there," he said.

"No, I didn't." Her sigh was heavy—not with defiance, but

with regret. "I just—I don't know."

Her voice caught and slipped through the crack in the barely-there light from the dash.

He glanced toward her, though not enough to risk crossing the line in the road. Her profile was illuminated by the pale moonlight from the windshield: a tight frown, eyes blank and burning at the same time.

"You had that look," he said.

"What look?"

He gestured vaguely with one hand. "The 'I'm one stray thought away from launching a spatula at your face' look."

A twitch flickered at the corner of her mouth, almost. Then it disappeared, replaced again by silence. Each second felt louder than the last.

Lincoln's thoughts folded inward, measured and filed, then emerged as a single entity.

"You think I don't care. About the past. About..." He stopped. His hand tensed around the wheel. "About us."

When she didn't answer, it was confirmation.

"That's not true." But even as he said it, the sentence didn't sound right.

She turned to face him. Cautious. Guarded. Her voice low. "Then what is?"

He didn't move his eyes from the road, but his grip shifted, tighter, colder.

Candy watched his face. "To me, it looks like it doesn't take much for you to pack up and walk away."

The words were out. Not practiced. Not coded. Just truth, bitter at the edges.

"I don't just throw things away, Candy."

"Really? Could've fooled me." Beside him, she laughed, but there was no breath behind it. "The boxes you left at your parents for the dump may also disagree."

"Those were things." His breath pushed through tight nostrils. Jaw set, eyes narrowing just barely as he forced the next words between clenched teeth. "There's a difference between letting go and just not even caring."

"Sounds convenient."

"I'm serious." He inhaled deeply, grounding himself against the sting of accusation. "Letting go of what doesn't serve you—it's not careless. It's survival."

A muscle jumped in her jaw. Then she turned toward the window. Quiet. His head was tilted slightly, so all he could see was the blur of her reflection in the glass.

She whispered the next word like it tasted betrayal. "Necessary?"

It landed like an indictment.

The air grew thick. Between them, the engine hummed a soft, endless tone beneath the weight of everything neither of them could say.

He swallowed. "Is that what you think I'm doing?"

She didn't answer.

"Throwing this away?"

Still nothing.

His hand moved instinctively, his left hand easing off the wheel until his knuckles blanched. "You think I'm just going to leave?" Quieter. He hated how it sounded—uncertain, sharp-edged.

He looked at her then. Her hands sat frozen in her lap, etched with tension. Her shoulders were drawn tight beneath the fabric of her jacket. It was as if she wanted to disappear inward. As if her silence was safer than anything that might follow her honesty.

Lincoln turned his gaze forward, to the road ahead—dark, narrow, infinite. A single streetlamp shimmered above the next bend like a lighthouse going dim.

He didn't have the right formula for this. Didn't have a spreadsheet or numbers to tally up the damage caused today. What he had was a truth he hadn't planned to face tonight. This wasn't about pulling away; it was that he never knew how to stay.

She sat in the palpable silence and stared out the window as the scenery flew past.

"You want to tell me what's wrong?"

There was a bite behind it. Sharp enough to register as a challenge. A test. "You can tell me what's wrong!"

Lincoln's chest grew heavier.

Before he could respond, she pressed on: "Oh, gee, I don't know, Lincoln. Maybe it's the fact that we just found out Bradley stole my mother's recipe, entered it in Sweet Success, and now he's trying to run me out of my own business."

The edge in her voice was jagged. Desperate.

"That's not new data." He exhaled slowly. "We're already working on fixing it."

Her scoff wasn't loud, but it burned intensely. "You don't get it."

Something inside him tightened. Because even if he didn't

know what to say, being told he didn't understand struck something narrow and deep. "Then explain it to me."

She turned. Her eyes locked onto his. And for a moment, the fury transformed into something far more dangerous.

"People leave, Lincoln." Three simple words.

He kept his eyes forward, but they hit him low. Hard. "I didn't say I was leaving."

Her breath caught. "Didn't you?"

A red light appeared ahead. Lincoln gently slowed the car to a stop, the silence settling between them like a held breath.

He turned toward her fully. "Not today."

Her pain wasn't loud. It was in the stillness of her expression, the carefully drawn lines of her mouth, and the begging not to believe in hope again.

"We haven't tried to figure any of that out."

She didn't nod, didn't speak.

But the hurt in her eyes said everything.

"You think I'm the guy who shows up, offers a fix, and walks away when the dust settles." He studied her face through layers of wariness. She wasn't mad at him.

She was preparing for him to do what he hadn't already denied.

"You plan things, Lincoln."

That sentence. Low. Even. "You fix things, look at them like math problems. You can't tell me you haven't done the math here. Or that, usually, when the numbers balance, you leave."

Her voice wasn't cold. It was sincere. Exhausted.

She turned her head, almost a gesture. "I get Patty's Cakes back. I get stability. But you..." Her next breath shook. "You get to go back to your life somewhere else."

The light turned green.

He didn't move.

Couldn't.

He opened his mouth to offer clarity, but the words came out wrong. "That's not fair."

It sounded weak. Not because it lacked truth, but because it was insufficient.

Candy laughed softly, bitter and hollow. "Maybe not. Doesn't mean it's not true."

He looked at her—really looked—and saw how tightly she was holding herself together. How much the idea of loss wasn't just fear; it was familiarity.

"You—" He tried. Stopped.

Scrubbed a hand down his face.

His jaw clenched. "I'm not Bradley."

Even speaking the name felt like a snare. A reminder of every reason she had to doubt men like him.

"I trusted him."

His voice dropped into something rougher. "I'm not trying to hurt you."

Candy turned slightly toward him. Her mouth opened but didn't shake. One question lingered in the air like a thread between them. "Then why are you here?"

It was a plea. A prayer wrapped in someone else's voice.

He flexed his fingers.

She didn't want a hero; she wanted proof that there'd be more. She needed the illusion of permanence in a life built sideways.

He knew Candy wanted him to choose to stay. Not just because it was easy. Not because it was logical, but because she mattered.

With his hand on the wheel, even with his knuckles aching, he stared at the road ahead because Candy wasn't logic. She wasn't a pivot table. She was disorder, and worth losing control for, but the words wouldn't come.

The light changed. He pressed the gas, and as the car carried them forward, the air between them filled with everything he didn't yet know how to say.

And everything she already feared.

They pulled up to her apartment.

The engine ticked softly, heat pockets rising from the grilled hood into the still silence of the night. Inside the car, everything felt compressed—tight with unfinished thoughts, the kind of quiet weighted more by what hadn't been said than what had. Lincoln kept his hands gripped at ten and two, palms resting on smooth leather that now felt too slick.

She hadn't looked at him since the light turned green and they had coasted through that intersection—since her voice, brittle and low, had cut into him with the one question he couldn't answer neatly.

He turned his head and risked stealing a glance.

Candy faced forward, unmoving except for a small tremor in her pressed-together fingers clutching the hem of her sleeve. Her leg bounced slightly, a silent sign of the storm inside her.

Tension radiated from her like static electricity, with sharp edges and nerves jammed behind tired eyes.

She was already mourning, and he hadn't even left yet.

Lincoln turned toward her more fully. Words caught at the edge of his throat—dry, clumsy—and yet they still came out. "You're right about one thing."

Her lips tightened as her chin dipped infinitesimally. The way her muscles clenched—like bracing for impact—gnawed at his chest. "What's that?" she asked, voice wrapped in restraint.

Lincoln watched her. The soft glow of the streetlamp spilled through the windshield, highlighting the faint shadows beneath her eyes and casting light across her cheekbone. She looked tired in a way that had nothing to do with baking or business. Worn from hope worn too thin.

His jaw flexed. "I do like being here."

He said it too softly for it to seem like a big revelation, but the truth behind it hit harder than anything he'd planned to say. He hadn't meant the town or the bakery.

He'd meant in this car, this moment, with a woman who'd somehow made everything else feel worth staying for.

Candy's shoulders, curled into uncertain armor, shifted—with the smallest reflex of something terrifyingly vulnerable. Like she was daring to hope.

And he couldn't take it. Not with nothing concrete in his hands to offer back. He reached for the door handle, his fingers clumsy with urgency, and opened the door before the moment could escalate further.

The night air rushed in—cool, sharp, laced with honeysuckle from somewhere nearby. It cut across his cheeks as he rounded the hood, his footsteps too quick, boots dull against gravel. He didn't speak when he opened her door. He just stood back, fists clenched at his sides, to stop himself from reaching for her.

She slipped out of her seat slowly, quietly, as if she was still waiting for something he hadn't said yet.

He caught her gaze for a moment before stepping back. "Get some rest, Candy," he said softly, but with emotion. His voice revealed more than he intended, and then he turned away.

The driver's side door groaned open, then thunked shut with finality.

In the side mirror, her reflection hung suspended—backlit by her porch light. Not blinking. Not retreating. As if she thought that if she stood still long enough, he might come back.

His fingers tightened on the steering wheel so hard the leather creaked.

He didn't go back.

And as he drove away, white lines blurring beneath headlights, something inside stretched tight—an impossible thread anchored somewhere just behind him.

Chapter Twenty-One

Candy

She stood in the middle of Patty's Cakes, staring blankly at the mixing bowls and baking trays scattered across the counter. Her hands trembled slightly, her mind spinning with lingering echoes of her argument with Lincoln.

You think I'm just going to leave.

Didn't you?

Her chest tightened. She inhaled sharply, pressing her palms against the cool surface of the counter, but everything — the betrayal, the competition, losing Lincoln — continued to weigh on her.

The front door chimed.

Before she could move, Bailey strolled in, holding two paper cups with lids and wearing the determined expression of someone who had no intention of letting her wallow.

"You look like you're about to crawl into that mixing bowl and never come out." Bailey set one of the cups down in front of her. "Drink up before I start making terrible life choices on your behalf."

Candy blinked, momentarily thrown off. "What kind of terrible choices?"

"The kind involving your rival bakery, industrial-strength Saran Wrap, and a very large bucket of glitter." Bailey took a sip of coffee. "I'll let you fill in the blanks."

Despite the weight pressing on her ribs, Candy let out a laugh and grabbed the cup. Warmth seeped into her fingers, grounding her just enough. "Thanks."

Bailey looked at her over the rim of her cup. "Alright. Now that I've momentarily saved you from caffeine withdrawal—want to tell me why you're standing in your own bakery looking like an abandoned pie on a discount rack?"

"I need to perfect this recipe and send it to the judges by tomorrow morning." Candy looked down at the half-mixed batter in front of her and exhaled slowly.

And that's nothing new, and you're almost there," Bailey said while picking at a patty cake sample. "I think it's great.

"It's great, but it's not *special*."

"Hun, you're being hard on yourself."

Candy mixed the batter with a few more thoughtful turns. "Lincoln and I had a fight."

Bailey nodded knowingly. "And, now you're spiraling."

"I'm not spiraling."

Bailey gave her a practiced mom stare.

Candy groaned, dragging a hand through her hair. "Okay, fine. I'm spiraling a little."

"There you go." Bailey leaned in. "Progress."

Candy sighed. "I just...I don't know how to fix this."

Bailey set her coffee down and crossed her arms. "Lincoln or the cake?"

Candy squirmed. "Both."

"Well, good news," Bailey said, giving the mixing bowl a pointed look. "One of those things is sitting right in front of you and actually wants to cooperate."

Candy hesitated, gazing at the batter...the half-finished, incomplete promise of something better.

Her mother's voice echoed in the back of her mind.

Your Patty Cake is special because you make it with love.

Candy inhaled sharply. That was it. That was the missing piece. Not just the technique or the ingredients, but *her*.

Her mother had never been afraid to experiment, to trust her instincts. Every cake, every recipe had been a reflection of who she was—her adventurous spirit and her passion for life.

Candy had started this competition trying to preserve her mother's legacy, but maybe she had been forgetting to make it *hers*.

Her pulse steadied. "I need to bake."

Bailey grinned. "Now, we're talking."

Candy reached for her apron, slipping it over her head, already recalculating. "The brown butter deepens the flavor, and the lavender is unique, but it needs something to balance the flavors."

Bailey hopped onto a stool, watching. "What are you thinking?"

Candy scanned the shelves, rolling her bottom lip between her teeth. Then her gaze landed on a small glass jar near the back. Honey.

A slow grin spread across her lips. "We tried to find a ratio for the sweetness with honey."

"Ooh. Like, a light glaze?" asked Bailey.

"No," Candy murmured, grabbing the jar. "In the batter. Half sugar, half honey. It made the texture smoother, and the cake richer, but it overpowered the lavender a bit."

"You're feeling it now, huh?" Bailey smirked. "So, you need something on the opposite end of honey."

Candy nodded, grabbing a second ingredient. "Lemon zest—just a little."

Bailey snagged a whisk, handing it to her. "Keep going."

The perfect ingredients were coming together for her. Candy moved with purpose. She folded the honey into the batter, the smooth richness blending seamlessly with the browned butter. Then, she prepared an icing with lavender and a citrus zest, brightening the entire mixture.

Bailey stepped back, watching with quiet satisfaction.

Ten minutes later, the cakes had gone into the oven.

As the scent started filling the kitchen, Candy leaned against the counter, feeling warm and steady.

Bailey nudged her with her elbow. "Welcome back."

Candy smiled, feeling the tension in her shoulders ease. "I'm winning this."

Bailey smirked. "Hell yes, you are."

Candy inhaled deeply as the timer counted down, finally feeling ready for Sweet Success.

Five minutes. Five more minutes until she could pull out her own Patty Cake out of the oven. Candy wiped her hands on a dish towel and stared at the timer as it counted down.

She'd made a few modifications after Bailey left. With careful measurement and adjustments, she'd perfected the rise and density. There were no other changes needed. It was perfect, and a version Bradley would never be able to replicate.

Yet, even as the bakery filled with a hint of warm honey and lavender, something still felt wrong. Not just something. Someone.

She exhaled, fidgeting with her apron. Lincoln hadn't been back since he dropped her off last night. She told herself she wasn't bothered by his absence, that their argument hadn't hurt her, but the tightness pressing against her ribs told a different story.

The bakery door chimed.

Her pulse kicked.

She turned just in time to see Lincoln stepping inside.

For half a second, she just stared. He looked the same—crisp button-down, sleeves pushed up to his elbows like he had just come from a long day of making sensible decisions, but something in his posture was different. Less rigid. More hesitant. His eyes flicked to the oven before settling on her.

Candy swallowed. "I didn't expect to see you here."

Lincoln nodded toward the timer ticking down. "I heard you had a breakthrough."

She raised an eyebrow. "Bailey?"

He let out a soft laugh. "Bailey."

Candy crossed her arms, her pulse pounding. "You sure you

want to be here? Wouldn't want you to get too…attached."

The words were meant as teasing. Instead, they betrayed something else.

Lincoln crossed the room in three measured steps, stopping just in front of her. "You think I don't care?" His voice was quiet, controlled.

Candy held his gaze. "I don't…I don't know."

Lincoln didn't move. "I do care." He said it evenly. "This isn't just a checklist for me, Candy. You aren't just something I plan to fix and walk away from."

Her breath hitched.

Lincoln frowned slightly, like he was realizing the depth of his own words in real-time.

The timer dinged, but they both held still.

Then, after a long beat, Candy whispered, "I should get that."

Lincoln nodded, stepping back as she turned toward the oven. He didn't leave, didn't retreat into distance or silence. He just stood there, watching her pull out the tray.

The first thing she noticed was the color.

It was golden, rich, and perfectly right.

Holding her breath, she lifted one from the pan and broke it open. Steam curled into the air, teasing her senses with warm honey and a savory sweetness.

She hesitated for a moment before tearing off a small piece, dipping an edge in the bowl of icing nearby, and handing it to Lincoln.

He took it, his fingers brushing against hers—warm and lingering.

Then, slowly, he chewed.

Candy held her breath.

For several agonizing seconds, Lincoln's face stayed blank, his analytical mind likely dissecting flavors like a scientist.

Then—

Something in his expression shifted. His lips quirked, just barely. He swallowed. Looked at her. And then, with a slow nod, he said, "That's it."

Candy didn't realize she was holding her breath until she exhaled quickly. "Yeah?"

Lincoln nodded again. "Yeah."

A slow grin spread across her lips. She had done it. *They* had done it.

The relief hit her so hard she barely had time to register the warmth in Lincoln's gaze before he stepped closer and pulled her in for a kiss.

It wasn't hesitant this time. He wasn't testing the waters or weighing a risk. It was certainty, a conviction, and it was the quiet answer to a question they hadn't been brave enough to ask. By the time they pulled apart, her heart was pounding, and his forehead was resting lightly against hers.

"Maybe," she murmured, breathless, "we had the secret ingredient all along."

Lincoln released a shaky chuckle, his hand still resting at her waist. "I told you structure was important."

Candy smirked, brushing her thumb against his jaw. "Pretty sure I was the one who said magic exists in the mess."

His lips twitched, and then he kissed her again.

Candy pulled him closer. She had a plan. She had her recipe, and now, she had him, too.

Chapter Twenty-Two

Candy

She lay curled against Lincoln, absently tracing slow, lazy circles over his chest through the soft cotton of his T-shirt. The steady rise and fall beneath her hand calmed her, the warmth of him anchoring her in the quiet. Late-night shadows stretched across the couch, and the world outside her apartment felt a thousand miles away. She tilted her head up, eyes thoughtful and searching.

"Do you think we'll win?" she whispered.

He smiled, his hand sliding up her bare arm. "I think your Patty Cake will be the best thing there."

She nudged him, lips curling. "Our Patty Cake."

Her thoughts drifted to how their recipe had come together as a blend of everything she loved: the rich, nutty brown butter that reminded her of her community's deep flavors, the lavender from Lincoln's family, her mother's Patty Cake legacy, and her own bright hint of lemon. It was all the pieces of her life, folded into something entirely new.

"If you'd asked me a year ago—hell, six months ago—what I'd be doing now, I never would've said baking for a contest or eating purple foods," he admitted, voice low and warm.

Candy feigned mock outrage. "They're good for you."

He chuckled, tightening his arm around her and pulling her closer. "You're good for me."

She laughed softly as he shifted, guiding her onto her back until he hovered just above her, the couch dipping beneath their weight. His body pressed gently against hers. It felt solid and reassuring, not heavy. He dipped down, brushing a kiss to her forehead, then another along her cheek, and one more at the corner of her mouth.

She shivered at the softness of it all—the gentle warmth of his breath, the steady beat of his heart against her ribs.

"Are you ready for Sweet Success tomorrow?" He asked, his voice a quiet murmur against her skin.

"Probably?" Her laugh trembled slightly, nerves showing through. Memories of the long week flickered behind her eyes: the late nights, every recipe test, every moment she'd second-guessed herself. But with Lincoln's weight grounding her and his fingers tracing lazy lines along her shoulder, the anxiety started to ease.

When he lifted his head, she found him watching her with that open expression she'd come to crave—equal parts admiration and quiet certainty.

He touched his forehead to hers, their noses brushing. "Let me help you forget about tomorrow for a while," he whispered.

She tilted her mouth up, smiling softly as he kissed her slowly, but insistently. One hand found the back of his neck, fingers threading through his hair. The other slid up his arm, feeling the strength there, the steadiness. He kissed her again, and again, each kiss a little deeper, until she was laughing softly into his mouth.

Lincoln took his time, brushing his thumb along her jaw, then down her arm to tangle their fingers together. He kissed her temple, her nose, the curve of her smile. She let herself melt into it, legs tangled with his as they sank further into the couch cushions. The quiet hum of the city outside felt impossibly far away.

He nuzzled her neck, his lips barely grazing her skin. "You're shaking," he murmured with a teasing grin.

"That's your fault," she whispered, laughter threading through her voice.

He pressed a kiss just below her ear, his voice low but gentle. "I could get used to this."

Her answer came soft and sure. "Me too."

They stayed like that for a long time, trading slow kisses and whispered jokes. Eventually, Candy sighed, tracing another lazy heart on his chest. He caught her hand and pressed a kiss to her knuckles, smiling against her skin.

Her heart softened. The tight knot of worry that had followed her all week finally began to ease. Each night she spent like this, in the circle of his arms, she felt a little steadier.

Chapter Twenty-Three

Candy

As Candy entered the grand event hall for the Sweet Success competition, she adjusted the bow on the apron Taylor had given her. The space was large, with sterile steel workstations lining the room under bright studio lights. The air buzzed with the quiet energy of contestants setting up their stations, and cameras hovered like watchful eyes, capturing pre-show footage.

Lincoln walked beside her, calm but still glancing around with slight uncertainty and careful inspection. "No cutting corners here," he murmured.

"No," Candy agreed, swallowing the hard knot of nerves in her throat. "It doesn't appear so."

This was it—the moment they had been working towards. The moment that could change everything for Patty's Cakes.

Candy squared her shoulders.

Then, a voice she'd rather never hear again cut through the hum of conversation.

"Well, would you look at that. You actually showed up."

Candy and Lincoln turned together.

Bradley stood a few feet away, his chef's jacket perfectly pressed, with the logo for The Mulberry Café neatly embroidered across the front. His relaxed, practiced smirk made Candy's hands form fists before she forced herself to relax them.

Beside her, Lincoln stiffened.

Candy forced a sweet smile. "Bradley, I know you love the sound of your own voice, but save some of that hot air—you'll need it when you're trying to figure out how to explain your inevitable loss."

The smirk didn't falter; in fact, it only grew sharper. "Feisty," he mused. "I'll give you that, but confidence alone won't save Patty's Cakes."

Lincoln's presence subtly moved closer to her side. "You'd know all about winning with other people's work."

Bradley's smirk flickered for a moment before smoothing out. Then, with an irritating level of ease, he tilted his chin. "I'm just saying, Candy, maybe stepping into a competition like this was a bit ambitious."

Candy's jaw flexed, but before she could unleash the storm brewing inside her, the overhead speaker crackled to life.

"Welcome, bakers, to the Sweet Success competition!"

The contestants fell into hushed attention.

The next two days will challenge every part of your skills—from accuracy and consistency to speed and creativity. You'll go beyond your limits and reach greatness.

A ripple of quiet anticipation moved through the room.

Lincoln nudged her side.

Candy inhaled and let go of the tension in her shoulders.

"We begin with your first challenge: Create a signature dessert that captures the heart and soul of your bakery."

Something inside of Candy stilled.

"The dessert must reflect your core philosophy. What makes your work stand apart? What tells your story? You'll have two hours to present your creation."

A murmur of conversation ran through the room as the contestants began adjusting their stations.

Lincoln nodded. "Not the Patty Cake."

"Not yet," Candy said, steeling herself. "Mom's Brambleberry Tartlets." Her fingers hovered over the stack of ceramic bowls before carefully plucking one up. "It was the first recipe she taught Bailey and me how to make when she opened Patty's Cakes."

Lincoln nodded once, firm and deliberate. He followed her movement, swiftly washing his hands and pulling out utensils. "So, this is about—"

"Family. Community. Patty's Cakes was never just mine. Mom built it with love, but people like Bailey and the community of Serenity were a part of it from the beginning." Candy cracked an egg into the bowl, hands moving with the grace of long-practiced muscle memory.

Lincoln nodded, already sifting flour. "What makes the tartlets stand out?"

Candy gathered fresh blackberries and raspberries, then mixed them with sugar in a small saucepan. "The filling. It's bright, tangy, sweet, but not overly so. My Mom always used a blend of citrus zest and a touch of vanilla bean to give it depth."

"The technical part?"

"The crust." Candy exhaled, pulling out a rolling pin. "A perfect pâte sucrée. It's delicate and buttery, but structured enough to hold the filling. Making it flaky without being brittle is the challenge."

Lincoln hummed, watching her expertly shape the dough into perfect circles. "And you and Bailey made this with your mom?"

Candy nodded, carefully pressing the dough into small tart molds. "On our first day in the bakery, my mom taught us how to tell if the dough was ready with just our fingertips. Bailey was nervous because she had never made pastry before. But my mom simply guided her hands over the dough and said, 'Baking is about trust. Trust your hands, trust your instincts, and when and if you mess up? We fix it.'"

"Sounds familiar." Lincoln's eyes flickered with something unreadable. "So, this isn't just a signature recipe; it's part of your history."

Candy's breath hitched at the way he said it—like he truly understood what this meant to her. "Yes," she said softly.

Lincoln kept his hands moving, his motions swift but precise, and she was struck again by how effortlessly they worked together. They'd become a team.

Across the kitchen, Bradley's voice rang out, smooth and practiced enough for cameras to pan toward him.

I, for one, can't wait to introduce the judges to my Mulberry Heritage Pie. It's a treasured recipe that embodies the heart of The Mulberry Café's legacy. His tone was casual, effortless.

Candy's hands froze mid-motion.

Her heart stuttered as she turned toward him to look at

what was happening in his workstation. Heritage Pie. Not just any pie. *Her mother's Blue Ribbon Pecan Bourbon Pie.*

The one her mom had made every year for the county fair, the one that had won the grand prize more times than Candy could count, and the only time it had ever been written down was in her mother's weathered recipe notebook, as her memory had started to fade.

The notebook Bradley had stolen.

Bradley caught her stare and smiled—easy, deliberate, taunting.

Candy's fingers curled into her apron. He had taken another piece of her mother's legacy, and whether or not the judges knew, *Candy did.*

Bradley cast a quick glance toward her station, his lips curling up just a bit. The challenge was silent.

And maybe, on any other day, she would have let it go, but not today. She met his eyes with a knowing smile. "Interesting choice," she mused, her tone light. "It feels...familiar."

Several contestants turned their heads, subtly observing the exchange.

Bradley grinned, slow and deliberate.

One of the judges cocked an interested brow.

Lincoln exhaled something close to a laugh beside her.

Then, before Bradley could fire back, the host clapped her hands.

"Alright, bakers! Your two hours start...NOW!"

Candy blocked out everything else. She tied her apron tighter and locked eyes with Lincoln. "Let's bake."

The competition kitchen buzzed with energy as contestants moved quickly at their stations, the atmosphere alive with organized chaos. The sharp sound of knives chopping and the steady hum of mixers filled the space, while bright overhead lights intensely highlighted every detail. Unlike the warm comfort of Patty's Cakes, this kitchen focused on precision, effort, and the intense focus of perfectionists under pressure.

Candy inhaled slowly, steadies herself as her prep time begins. Everything had led to this moment.

The contestant stations were set up in a half-circle, each with gleaming steel counters and fully stocked with top-quality ingredients. Cameras quietly hovered above, capturing every moment as they baked, while the judges walked around the perimeter, their keen eyes watching each competitor carefully.

Bradley worked at a station across from Candy with his usual air of arrogance. He wasn't alone; Sabrina had joined him. Her movements were sharp and precise as she adjusted their workstation. Unlike Bradley, she wasn't playing to the cameras—her focus was serious and professional. There was no smirk on her lips, no gloating.

Candy caught Bradley's gaze just as he gave her a slow, knowing smirk—the classic "Why do you even try?" expression that had haunted her for too long.

Lincoln, standing beside her and already scanning their station, noticed the exchange. "The Countdown Clock starts in two minutes," he murmured.

Candy straightened, rolling her shoulders back. "I know."

Lincoln met her gaze, his quiet, unwavering confidence rooting her in place. "You ready?"

Candy blew out a slow breath. "No." She exhaled again. "Yeah."

His mouth twitched, but he had no chance to reply—the pre-show speakers crackled overhead:

"Bakers, your first challenge starts...now!"

A rapid movement burst from each station, but Candy's focus sharpened as she reached for her ingredients. Their brambleberry tartlets had to be perfect. Crisp yet tender crust, designed to support the filling without cracking. One misstep, one moment of hesitation, could ruin everything.

Lincoln worked alongside her, portioning and preparing as if he were an extension of her thoughts. They moved in perfect sync. When she reached for the cinnamon, he was already handing it to her. When she needed the whisk, he nudged it a little closer without looking up.

Across the room, Sabrina worked with the same quiet efficiency, with precision in her movements, eyes narrowed as she leveled flour into a measuring cup. Bradley, on the other hand, wasn't paying attention at all. He kept flicking smug glances at Candy, his focus slipping away from the task at hand.

Lincoln noticed. "He's distracted. That's going to cost him."

Candy smirked, rolling out her dough. "Good."

From the corner of her eye, she saw Sabrina's head jerk toward Bradley, an impatient flicker crossing her expression.

"He's showing off for you," she muttered, just loud enough for Candy to catch.

Candy blinked, surprised.

Sabrina didn't meet her gaze, just continued rolling out pastry dough with firm, purposeful movements. Then she muttered something under her breath that Candy couldn't quite hear, but whatever it was made Bradley's expression tighten.

Interesting. Perhaps there was trouble in paradise.

Candy ignored them, turning back toward her own work. The fruit filling simmered in its pan, releasing waves of warm berry and citrus-sweet vanilla. The scent curled through the air like nostalgia itself, and she didn't miss the way Lincoln—steady, logical, data-focused Lincoln—closed his eyes for just a second, inhaling deeply.

This is the part where I say baking is art, not numbers," she teased.

He exhaled sharply through his nose, but she saw the twitch of amusement he was trying to hide. "I'll allow it."

She grinned.

The oven timer beeped, pulling her back to the moment.

Lincoln pulled out the first batch of tart crusts—golden, delicate, a promise of perfection.

Candy barely had time to celebrate before her elbow knocked into the cooling rack. The tray tipped, her stomach plunged, a sharp inhale behind her, and then Lincoln's hand shot out, catching it before disaster struck.

A breath of relief shuddered through her.

"You're a lifesaver," Candy muttered, her pulse still racing.

Lincoln carefully set the tray down, not even looking at her as he murmured, "Eh, I'm more than just an accountant."

Still shaken, she huffed out a breath. "I'm starting to figure that out."

The final minutes bled away in a rapid haze of plating, garnishing, and perfectly timed execution.

"Thirty seconds," the announcer called.

Lincoln slid the last plate forward as Candy piped a careful swirl of vanilla bean whipped cream atop each tart, the finishing touch delicate but intentional.

All around them, rushed movements and frantic hands scrambled to pull everything together. Across the way, Bradley glanced up at the timer, his brows knitting together just slightly.

Sabrina, however, was still moving with perfect precision, head down, finishing their plating. She turned to grab the piping bag, only to realize Bradley was still holding it, his smirk fading. She exhaled sharply through her nose and quickly fumbled to finish their recipe.

"Five...four...three..."

Candy smiled at Lincoln, reaching for his hand.

He squeezed her fingers once, solid and steady.

"Two...one...time."

The loud buzz signaled the end of the challenge.

Candy stepped back, her chest rising and falling as adrenaline surged through her, her heart pounding. From the corner of her vision, she saw movement—Bradley lowering his piping bag just a second too late.

Chapter Twenty-Four

Candy

The competition kitchen buzzed with nervous energy as the judges moved through the room, clipboards in hand. The smell of cookies and cakes thickened the air, mingling with the low murmur of competitors adjusting their plating and utensils clinking against porcelain.

Candy stood beside Lincoln at their station, her grip firm around the hem of her apron, the adrenaline still thrumming through her veins. She had never been much for waiting, and standing there as the judges approached made her stomach twist into knots.

The lead judge, a distinguished woman with silver-streaked hair and sharp eyes, reached for one of Candy's brambleberry tartlets. She examined it carefully, her gaze following the golden crust, the glossy berry filling, and the delicate swirl of vanilla-bean whipped cream.

Then, with a deliberate patience that made Candy want to climb out of her skin, she took a bite. The room seemed to hold its breath. One second passed, and another.

Then, her brows raised, her lips pressed together in surprise. She took another bite, and with a nod, she turned to the second judge. "The crust is exceptional," she mused. "Flaky, structured, but it melts the very moment it hits your tongue."

Another judge hummed in agreement, taking a second bite of his own tartlet. "The filling is also bright, well-balanced. The citrus ties it together beautifully."

Lincoln remained still, his hands in his pockets, in what Candy knew was his perfected form of careful observation. But underneath that, she could sense the quiet support she'd come to appreciate so much.

Finally, the silver-haired judge turned to Candy, curiosity flickering in her eyes. "Tell me, Miss Malone," she said, "what inspired this dessert?"

Candy straightened, forcing herself to ignore the burn of Bradley's eyes on her from two stations away. "This was my mother's. I grew up baking it with her and my best friend, so it's the first thing I ever learned to make as a kid."

The judge offered a rare, appreciative smile. "Well, then that explains why it tastes like home."

Candy held her breath. The moment felt like a significant validation not just of her skill, but of the legacy she was fighting to protect.

The judges finished their final notes and stepped away. Candy barely had time to process the relief before Lincoln leaned in and muttered, "Watch."

Candy tracked his line of sight.

Bradley.

The next judge reached for one of Bradley's pecan bourbon tartlets. It was the same dessert her mother had taken home blue ribbons for at the county fair for nearly a decade straight. The glossy pecans sat atop the caramelized filling, looking perfect. But Candy knew better—presentation meant nothing if you couldn't deliver.

The judges took their first bites. Unlike before, no one reacted immediately. One nodded a few times, pressing his lips together. Another hummed, grabbing his fork again, this time nudging the crust.

"The flavors are solid," the judge finally said, his tone controlled. "But the crust…" He shook his head slightly. "It's dense and a little too dry."

Candy didn't move. But inside? Oh, she was grinning.

The silver-haired woman looked up and set down her fork. "Bourbon pecan pies are a staple of Southern baking, and they require an extremely deft hand."

Bradley's smirk barely faltered as he delivered his practiced charm. "I believe in honoring tradition. I wanted to craft something familiar that stood strong in its roots."

Another judge hummed thoughtfully. "The flavors are there," he admitted, nudging the crust again. "But the balance is off."

Bradley's jaw twitched. Candy barely noticed it—the way his fingers tightened slightly around the pastry bag before he forced them to relax.

Sabrina, however, didn't react at all. She didn't flinch. She didn't step in with the easy deference of a business partner smoothing things over. She just kept her hands moving, her expression unreadable.

Bradley recovered quickly, smiling. "I appreciate the feedback."

The judges started walking toward the next table. One judge gave him a final polite nod and jotted down a note before continuing.

As they turned away, Sabrina reached for something on their station, or at least, she started to. Her hand barely grazed the counter before stopping mid-motion, her lips pressing together in a sharp line.

Candy didn't hear the word Sabrina muttered under her breath, but whatever it was, Bradley's entire posture changed. It wasn't an immediate snap. Not an explosion, but something slower. Like a coil winding too tightly, Sabrina's shoulders lifted just slightly on her next inhale.

Bradley turned to look at her, no longer smiling.

Candy exchanged a quick glance with Lincoln.

He had noticed it too. "They're off," he murmured, adjusting his glasses, his focus locked on the two of them. "Something's changed."

Candy nodded slightly, trying to pinpoint *what* exactly that something was.

Sabrina's jaw tightened, but she avoided looking at Bradley directly. She simply reached for the cooling rack, her fingers gripping the edge with a bit too much precision, as if she needed something to keep her grounded.

Bradley kept his grip tight on the piping bag for two seconds too long before exhaling through his nose and setting it down.

"Whatever that was," Lincoln murmured, "it wasn't nothing."

Candy hummed, turning back toward her own station, but not before catching the sharp, clipped motion of Sabrina fixing their tools on the counter. She didn't know what had just unraveled between them, but something told her this wouldn't be their last moment of silence. "No." She said, "It wasn't."

The judges finished their rounds, stepping back toward the front of the room to deliver the first results.

Candy's breath caught as the rankings lit up on the screen behind them.

1st Place: Candy Malone – Brambleberry Tartlets

2nd Place: Bradley Tanner – Bourbon Pecan Tart

3rd Place: Jenna Michaels – Honey Citrus Madeleines

Applause rippled through the room. Candy's hands trembled slightly at her sides.

She had won the first round.

Bradley placed second.

And, based on the dark flicker in his expression when he glanced back at the screen, he did not take it well. Neither did Sabrina.

She didn't need to be psychic to see what was coming.

Bradley wasn't just frustrated. He was furious, and it looked like Sabrina was *done*.

Lincoln leaned in, his voice low. "He's going to come for you after this."

Candy didn't hesitate.

She straightened her shoulders, tilting her chin. "Let him."

The Sweet Success competition break room was unnervingly quiet—a stark contrast to the controlled chaos of the main kitchen. Candy sat rigidly on a stool, fingers clenched around a cup of water she had yet to drink. The first round was over. She had won.

And she wasn't foolish enough to think Bradley would just accept that.

She had seen it in his eyes the second the leaderboard flashed her name above his. They'd contained fury, tightly coiled beneath that practiced confidence.

Lincoln skimmed the competition schedule taped to the wall. "Round two is technical," he murmured. "'Back to the Basics.'"

Candy swallowed, pulse steadying. "I'm going with a simple sourdough roll." It wasn't the easiest challenge, but she had planned for it. "The starter is prepped and proofing. We should be good."

Lincoln hummed in agreement, but his glance toward the door was sharp and wary. He was always analyzing, always assessing variables.

Candy had a sinking feeling that the variable had a name.

The door swung open.

Bradley.

Speak of the devil.

His posture was languid, too casual for a man still recovering from second place. He strolled across the room to the water station as if he had all the time in the world. Candy knew better.

When Bradley looked relaxed, it meant he was already a step ahead.

"Nice job out there," Bradley said, screwing the cap off a bottle of water. "You almost looked like you knew what you were doing."

Candy smiled sweetly, though her grip on her water cup tightened. "How about that? Turns out I just might."

Lincoln, standing beside her, stayed perfectly still. His silence might have made most people uncomfortable, but Bradley wasn't most people. His smirk stayed as he took a slow sip from his water bottle before looking around. "Where's Sabrina?"

Bradley frowned slightly. "She couldn't stay."

"Oh, she left?"

Bradley exhaled, rolling his shoulders. "Yeah. Something urgent came up with the bakery, apparently." He made a show of checking his watch. "She rushed out like it was life or death. Didn't give me much of a choice but to handle things myself."

Candy and Lincoln exchanged a brief, knowing glance, too quick for Bradley to catch.

He continued, oblivious. "It's fine, though. I've got everything under control," he drawled. "She'll be kicking herself when she finds out she missed the moment I take first place."

Lincoln arched a brow but didn't comment.

Candy forced another smile, keeping her tone deceptively light. "Well, isn't that lucky for you?"

Bradley flashed another smirk, all teeth. "That's what I keep telling her."

Lincoln took a slow sip from his water bottle. "Mm."

Bradley didn't seem to notice the clipped edge of that single sound. Instead, he straightened, exuding confidence. Bradley flicked his gaze lazily back to Candy. "Looking forward to round two. I hope you're ready."

Cold dread curled in Candy's gut.

Lincoln's entire body stilled. "Why?"

Bradley shrugged, rolling his shoulders. "No reason. Just wouldn't want any…unexpected setbacks."

A slow, calculated wink, and then he turned and strutted toward the refreshment table.

Candy fought the urge to roll her eyes. She waited until he was out of earshot before looking up at Lincoln. "Something tells me she didn't rush off to deal with 'bakery issues'," she murmured.

Lincoln hummed thoughtfully. "No. I imagine she finally decided he's the one who's the issue."

Candy exhaled. "If that's the case, this is about to get interesting."

Lincoln stayed silent because he didn't need to speak. They both understood that Bradley's ego was already hurt from coming in second in the first round. If Sabrina had really walked out?

That wound was about to bleed, and Candy was more than ready to watch him spin out.

"Where is the sourdough starter?" Candy asked, her stomach sinking.

They had left it sealed in a ceramic bowl beneath the counter before the break. It was supposed to be right there, but the proofing box was empty.

A cold prickle raced up the back of her neck.

"Tell me you moved it," she said, even as a sinking feeling told her otherwise.

Lincoln checked the space again, more out of logic than hope. Then he exhaled sharply. "I didn't."

Candy's fists clenched at her sides. "That son of a—"

Across the kitchen, Bradley stood at his station watching them.

Smiling.

Candy saw red.

"This was our core ingredient." Her voice was sharp, cutting. "He knew that."

"Which is exactly why he wanted it gone," Lincoln said. His tone was calm, but Candy had worked with him long enough to sense the controlled anger just beneath the surface.

They could report to the judges or file an official complaint about tampering, but they had no proof. No one had seen Bradley remove anything, and he was clever enough not to leave any evidence.

If they wasted their time fighting this, they'd lose the round by default.

And Bradley knew it.

Candy exhaled hard. "He wants me to panic."

"You're not going to."

"New plan." She turned toward Lincoln.

Lincoln tilted his head. "You're sure?"

"No, but we don't have time to dwell on that." She exhaled quickly and sharply. "Sourdough's out, so we pivot. We need another base that can develop flavor fast...buttermilk biscuits?"

Lincoln's mind was already catching up. "Sour tang, and a little more reliable rise."

Candy nodded. "It won't have the same flavor, but we can get the right structure if we balance the fat content right."

Lincoln pressed his lips together, scanning the ingredient options again. "What do you need?"

Candy looked back at Bradley.

He still had that smug little look on his face. Her blood boiled. What she *wanted* was to walk over there and wipe that smirk off his face, but what she *needed* was victory.

She turned away, concentrating on what really mattered. "Flour. Cream cheese. A dash of cornstarch. We're going to make this work."

Lincoln nodded once, decisive. "Then let's do it."

Chapter Twenty-Five

Candy

Her hands moved swiftly, fingers pressing into the cool dough, rolling and shaping it with steady precision. It wasn't the sourdough she had planned, and wasn't the recipe she had spent weeks perfecting, but it didn't matter.

She could make this work. She had to.

Lincoln worked alongside her, measuring and leveling the ingredients she called out without hesitation, his efficiency preventing her from spiraling. There was a quiet, unspoken trust between them, an understanding that neither needed to explain.

He had her back.

Candy cast a quick glance across the competition kitchen, ignoring the frantic movements of other bakers. Bradley remained cool, calm, and collected. He knew exactly what he had done. He understood that sabotage couldn't be proved, and even worse, he knew that even if she suspected something, she wouldn't have had enough time to test or refine it.

Too bad for him, Candy thrived under pressure.

The biscuit dough came together, soft yet firm, just as she wanted. She sliced clean, even rounds, arranging them on the tray in tight, uniform rows.

Lincoln barely glanced up from his clipboard. "So, are you going to glare at him all day, or are you going to beat him?"

Candy exhaled, a hint of a grin flickering at her lips. "Both."

Lincoln smirked. "Good answer."

The timer above the workstation counted down.

"Twenty-five minutes," the host's voice echoed through the loudspeaker.

A pit tightened low in Candy's stomach. She wasn't out of the woods yet. The biscuits would work, but they weren't complex enough to stand on their own. She needed an edge. A finishing touch that would elevate them beyond a simple replacement.

Lincoln watched her, sensing the shift in her expression. "What are you thinking?"

Candy chewed her bottom lip, scanning the ingredients.

What turns a biscuit into more than just a biscuit? What transforms something simple into something unforgettable?

Then an idea clicked.

She turned abruptly, hands moving without hesitation. "We need honey butter."

Lincoln was already opening a fresh stick of butter. "Sweet finish?"

"And caramelization." Candy grabbed a small saucepan and set it on the burner. "If we glaze them before baking, we'll add depth and a golden crust. It'll feel intentional, not improvised."

Lincoln nodded, quickly jotting something in his notes, but his voice remained calm. Confident. "That'll do it."

Candy exhaled, centering herself as she worked.

She didn't just want to fix the problem. She wanted to win.

Warm honey and butter curled in the air as the biscuits cooled. The golden tops glistened. They'd risen higher than expected, perfectly shaped.

Candy held her breath as the final seconds on the timer ticked down.

"Five...four...three..."

Lincoln stood beside her, arms crossed, observing the oven with his usual focus.

"Two...one...time!"

The loud buzzer signaled the end of the challenge.

Candy exhaled and stepped back just as the judges started moving through the kitchen, their expressions unreadable as they approached each station. She saw Bradley watching her from across the room, arms crossed lazily over his chest. That smirk. That insufferable, smug smirk.

He wanted to fluster her. Wanted her to feel like she barely made it through. She wasn't giving him that satisfaction.

The head judge reached her station first, the silver-haired woman from the last round. She glanced down at the biscuits, nostrils flaring slightly as the honey butter glaze gleamed under the bright lights.

"Interesting choice," she mused, picking one up and gently

breaking it apart. Steam rose from the center, revealing delicate layers.

Candy straightened her shoulders, clasping her hands in front of her. "These were an adaptation," she explained, her voice steady despite the tremor in her pulse. "A warm honey butter biscuit, designed to be both soft and structured—lightly crisp on the exterior, airy on the inside, with rich caramelization on the crust."

The judge took a bite. Then another.

A long pause.

Then, the silver-haired woman hummed, tilting her head slightly.

"Delicious," she admitted, dabbing her mouth with a napkin. "Excellent texture, and the honey adds a beautiful depth."

Candy's shoulders loosened slightly.

Then, the same judge set her plate down—not roughly, but with the kind of deliberate movement Candy had already learned to recognize. The slight narrowing of her eyes and the thoughtful press of her lips.

"It is, however, a departure from the assignment," she continued. "The challenge was Back to Basics. We wanted a focus on fundamentals—the precision in technique. Your biscuits are wonderful, but with the honey-glaze enhancement, they lean toward innovation rather than the refinement of a simple classic concept."

Candy stilled.

Another judge nodded in agreement. "The balance is remarkable, but at the end of the day, the challenge was about perfecting a foundational skill—not elevating it beyond its intent."

The silver-haired judge delivered the final note with a firm sense of finality. "For competition standards, this would be a standout in an innovation round. But today? It overcomplicated the task."

Candy's stomach dropped.

Bradley shifted from across the room, drawing attention back to his station as the judges approached him.

Candy forced herself to keep a neutral expression, trying not to let frustration seep in. Instead, she watched silently as the judges evaluated Bradley's submission: a rustic French bâtard. Simple. Classic.

Bland.

But...perfectly aligned with the challenge.

While one judge noted the crust was slightly underbaked on one side, another praised the technical aspects—how it followed the principles of a sturdy French loaf and how it met every requirement of the round.

Bradley had played it safe, and it had worked.

The leader-board flickered overhead, and then the contestants' names appeared:

1st Place: Bradley Tanner – Rustic French Batard

2nd Place: Candy Malone – Honey Butter Biscuits

3rd Place: Lea Scott – Classic Dinner Rolls

The names burned into Candy's vision, unwavering.

She had won the first round.

Now, Bradley had won the second.

Their score was tied.

Lincoln frowned slightly, a small shift in his stance—one of those subtle tells indicating he was frustrated. Not necessarily at her, but at this.

Bradley turned, his smirk slow, smug, easy.

Candy forced herself to stand her ground as he walked toward her, his posture as relaxed as ever. But there was something sharp beneath his satisfaction now—something smug and pointed.

He stopped just short of invading her space.

"Second place looks good on you, Malone," he mused, his voice pitched just loud enough. "Maybe next round, you should stick to the assignment instead of playing around."

Candy didn't blink. "Maybe next round, you should try minding your own business and keeping your hands to yourself."

Lincoln exhaled sharply, amused.

Bradley wasn't. His smirk flickered briefly, but he quickly regained his composure. "This is a game," he murmured. "And now, we both know I can beat you. See you in the final round." And with that, he turned and walked away.

Candy sharply inhaled through her nose.

Lincoln paused for a moment. Then, with a steady voice, he said, "It was the better dish."

Candy exhaled, not in relief but with measured frustration. "I know."

Lincoln tilted his head, observing her reaction. "Then what's the problem?"

She bristled, shaking her head. "The problem, Lincoln, is that it shouldn't have been."

His brows furrowed. "Candy—"

"I let him set the pace," she cut in, her voice sharp. "I let him dictate how I responded instead of owning the moment. I let him get in my head, and I messed up."

Lincoln sighed, rubbing his temple as he leaned against the counter. "We pivoted. We made the best choice under the circumstances."

Candy scoffed. "We adapted—which is exactly what you love, isn't it? Strategize, modify, plan around the problem. But Lincoln? We were never meant to be in that position in the first place."

His jaw tightened. "And what would you have preferred? That we reported it? We didn't have proof. It would've been your word against his, and we would have wasted more time arguing than baking."

"At least I would've done something!"

Lincoln straightened, arms crossing. "You did do something. You adjusted, worked through it, and still came in second. Not last. Second."

Candy flinched at the word, her pulse pounding as she looked at him. "You don't get it."

Lincoln's lips pressed into a firm line. "No, I do. You get emotional, and you let Bradley use that against you—"

"Emotional?" She let out a sharp, unbelieving laugh. "Wow. And how did you handle it, Lincoln? You let me make those honey butter changes. Encouraged it, even." She pointed at him.

"I trusted your instincts. You chose to adapt that recipe," Lincoln continued, voice still calm. "And I stood by that choice because I believed in you."

Candy blinked, the weight of his words hanging between

them. Then, slowly, she shook her head. "And yet, now I'm emotional?"

Lincoln inhaled through his nose, pausing before responding. When he spoke again, his voice was lower. Controlled. "No," he said carefully, his frustration bleeding through measured restraint. "I'm saying you're punishing me for trusting you."

Candy's breath caught in her throat.

Lincoln dropped the rag in his hands onto the counter and exhaled sharply. "You're pissed because we lost the advantage. Your trust issues with Bradley? Fine. I get that, but don't lump me in with him just because I didn't stop you from making a choice that you wanted to own."

Candy's pulse pounded in her ears. She swallowed, then aggressively wiped down her station with more pressure than needed.

Lincoln stayed quiet for a long moment—watching her, studying how tightly wound she was. Then, clearly done with dragging the moment out, he reached for his bag and grabbed his clipboard. "I'll help finish the cleanup."

Candy didn't respond.

They worked in tense silence, the noise of the competition kitchen filling the space with unspoken, sharp thoughts. Candy grabbed her bag, her fingers trembling slightly as she slid the strap over her shoulder. She couldn't stay here. Not for another second.

"I'm heading out," she muttered.

Lincoln exhaled slowly, as if he wanted to say something, but he only nodded, his grip tightening around his clipboard.

Candy made it halfway to the door before something caused her to stop. Her fingers hovered over the doorknob, and her throat grew tight.

Maybe this was it. Maybe this was the moment when everything cracked open, and they both admitted what this truly was.

She turned, just enough to meet his gaze. "I'd understand," she whispered, "if you wanted to be done with this."

Lincoln didn't answer right away.

Candy shoved open the door and stepped into the cool evening air. Her pulse pounded beneath her skin, but the tightness wasn't caused by the lingering adrenaline from the competition.

It was the silence.

His silence.

Because it meant Lincoln was considering it.

She kept walking, each step toward the parking lot heavier than the last. The crisp night air should have cleared her mind, but all it did was sharpen the uncertainty curling in her stomach.

Behind her, she heard the door swing shut.

Five seconds later, Lincoln followed.

Neither of them spoke as they crossed the pavement; the only sound between them was the muted thud-thud of their footsteps against the asphalt. The tension clung thick, stretched too tight between them, unspoken words hanging in the night like ghosts.

When they reached their cars, Candy hesitated by her door, fingers tightening around the handle.

Lincoln exhaled sharply beside her.

Slowly, she turned.

Their eyes met in the faint glow of the parking lot lamps. For a moment, just a fraction of a second, she thought he might say something, but instead, he simply gave a small, measured nod, and then he got into his car.

Candy swallowed the ache climbing up her throat, then nodded back.

She unlocked her door and slid inside, clutching the steering wheel with cold, aching fingers. She didn't look up as Lincoln's engine rumbled to life—didn't watch for taillights fading into the distance.

Chapter Twenty-Six

Candy

She'd messed up.

Candy exhaled as she rested her forehead against the steering wheel. She'd allowed Bradley to manipulate her feelings, the way she snapped at Lincoln, and, worst of all, the way she handed him an escape.

I'd understand if you wanted to be done with this.

Why did she say that? She practically pushed him out the door, and the worst part?

He hadn't fought her on it.

Her phone buzzed against the console, and for a fleeting second, she hoped it was Lincoln, but when she looked at the screen, his name wasn't there.

Bailey.

Candy hesitated, debating whether she had the energy for a conversation, before sighing and swiping to pick up. "Hey."

"You sound like you got hit by a rolling pin," Bailey said dryly. "What happened?"

Candy groaned, clutching the wheel. "We lost the second round."

Bailey sucked in a sharp breath. "What? How?"

Candy pressed her fingers against her temple, headache forming. "Bradley stole my sourdough starter."

"You have got to be kidding," Bailey snapped.

"Nope."

"And the judges just—"

"We couldn't *prove* it."

A muffled thunk on Bailey's end, probably something falling onto her countertop. "I swear to God, if I had been there—"

"I know," Candy muttered. "Me too."

Bailey huffed. "Get over here. Now. Because the only thing standing between me and a full-blown sabotage scheme is alcohol and baked goods."

Candy let out a weak laugh as she shifted into drive. "Already on my way."

Bailey's kitchen smelled like warm vanilla and citrus. As Candy stepped inside, Bailey was already at the counter, pouring two generously salted margaritas.

"No offense," Bailey said, sliding one toward her, "but you look like emotional roadkill."

"Thanks for that." Candy sighed, grabbing her glass. "Day one was rough."

Bailey took a sip. "Want to tell me what happened?"

Candy swirled the melting ice in her drink. "We won the first round, but before round two started, Bradley stole my starter, and I panicked. We pivoted with a honey butter biscuit, but it wasn't the core prompt. So Bradley won."

Bailey wrinkled her nose. "Ugh."

Candy exhaled sharply. "Yeah."

Bailey looked at her. "That's not what's truly bothering you, though."

Candy looked at the condensation sliding down her glass, her fingers tightening slightly.

Bailey waited.

Finally—softly—Candy admitted, "I fought with Lincoln."

Bailey shot her the most unbearably smug look over the rim of her glass. "Ohhh. So that's why you look like someone stole all your frosting spatulas."

"This is serious," Candy muttered. "I...I don't know if I totally destroyed things between us."

Bailey narrowed her eyes. "Honey, did you tell him his spreadsheets were useless, or his partitioning system wasn't actually efficient?"

Candy shot her a look. "No?"

"Then I assure you, he's not that mad."

Candy sighed. "I basically told him he was going to walk away."

Bailey rolled her eyes. "And?"

Candy gawked. "And? Bailey, I pushed him away."

"No, you tested him," Bailey corrected, tapping her glass. "There's a difference."

Candy swallowed. "You don't think I ruined it?"

Bailey studied her for a beat. "No," she said finally. "I don't."

Candy exhaled, gripping the counter. "Then why hasn't he called?"

Bailey's lips twitched like she was holding *so* much back. "Oh, sweetheart."

Candy groaned. "What?"

Bailey grabbed her phone from the counter and started scrolling. "You really think Lincoln is the kind of guy who's not stewing over this right now? No, he's trying to figure out how to fix it and what went wrong. That man is probably scrolling through an Excel file titled 'Reasons Why Candy and I Shouldn't Have That Fight Again.'"

Candy buried a groan in her hands. "That sounds...painf ully accurate."

Bailey snorted. "Which means there's still a chance."

Candy took a deep breath before nodding. She had bigger matters to concentrate on right now. Lincoln wasn't just a distraction—he was part of this fight. Her fight. And if last night had shown anything, it was that he was worth trusting, even if that scared her.

Bailey must have recognized the shift because she tapped her fingernails against her glass. "Speaking of the actual enemy in this story..."

Candy groaned. "Do we have to?"

Bailey arched a brow. "Unless you'd rather spend the next hour analyzing why you look like you just lost your best chance at something real with Lincoln."

Candy stiffened, gripping her own glass a little too tightly. "I don't want to talk about that, either."

"Mm-hmm." Bailey didn't push, but the look she gave Candy made it clear—they would be circling back to that topic later.

Instead, she grabbed her phone and tapped the screen. "I had Clinton dig a little deeper into Bradley's...activities."

Candy frowned, stirring the melting ice in her drink. "And?"

"No official updates yet, but Clinton's analyzing the situation more carefully," Bailey said, voice calm but deliberate. "You've been treating the symptoms, Candy. Trying to keep the bakery from falling apart because of what Bradley did to it, but you haven't taken a step back to see the bigger picture."

Candy exhaled. "Because if I look at the bigger picture, I'll have to fully acknowledge that he didn't just sabotage the bakery financially—he stole time, resources, hell, he stole everything that should have been going toward making this contest my only focus."

Her voice cracked slightly, and she hated that it did.

Bailey sat back, watching her.

Candy ran a hand through her hair, her frustration tightening into something sharper. "I should be able to be here. Fully. Without worrying if the bakery is going to collapse the second my back is turned." She inhaled sharply. "I should be with my mother—not spending what could be her final months scrambling to keep the business alive because he decided he deserved more than what he earned."

Bailey's expression softened, but there was still fire in her eyes. "You're carrying all the weight, and you still haven't received the reward."

Candy's hollow laugh fell flat. "Exactly."

Bailey set her phone down. "And what about Lincoln?"

Candy flinched, her hands tightening in her lap. "What about him?"

Bailey tilted her head. "Do you regret what happened between you two?"

Candy exhaled, pressing her fingers against her temples. "I don't know. It's not like he left, but I feel like...I ruined whatever trust we had."

Bailey didn't respond at first.

Then, carefully, she said, "You didn't ruin it, but you do need to make this better." Bailey's voice was quiet but certain. "Lincoln is not Bradley."

Candy swallowed hard, her throat tight. "I know."

"But you don't *believe* it."

Candy shut her eyes. She wanted to believe it, but the heaviness in her chest made it difficult.

Bailey set her phone aside and reached across the table, squeezing Candy's hand. "Look, you are fighting fires while Bradley dances around, acting like he's already won, but he hasn't won. You are still here. We are still here."

Something steadied in Candy's chest.

Bailey let go, her posture shifting into a more business-like stance. "I'll follow up with Clinton. If Bradley was pulling resources from your accounts, we need to know exactly what the legal consequences are."

Candy nodded tightly. "Lincoln also passed the bakery

records to a forensic accountant, but they haven't sent back a final report yet. With the contest ending tomorrow, I…" She swallowed. "I don't trust Bradley not to do something desperate."

"We need a move that isn't reactionary," Bailey said, voice sharp. "You've been patching the symptoms, but it's time we deal with the real problem."

Candy took a deep breath, feeling the certainty deep in her bones.

Tomorrow, she will finish the contest. Then what?

Chapter Twenty-Seven

Lincoln

His fingers gripped the steering wheel so tightly that the leather edges pressed into his skin. The morning light reflected off the windows of the large concrete building hosting the Sweet Success contest. Through the shimmering reflections, he could see silhouettes inside—contestants moving around, staff rushing to prepare, the building quietly vibrating with purpose.

Jackson was still parked outside, remaining stubbornly unwilling to move.

The engine had gone quiet half an hour ago, and yet his pulse hadn't slowed. It thudded low and steady beneath his ribs, not panicked—just persistent. Like something inside him refused to be ignored.

This wasn't the plan. Come to Serenity. Move his parents. Fix the numbers. Leave. That was the plan.

Not long evenings baking with her, telling jokes. Not remembering that food once meant something—the way it felt to create, not just calculate. The way it had felt to be understood, but now?

Now, he couldn't bring himself to walk into a building to find her. He took a deep breath, grabbed his phone from the passenger seat, and thumbed through his contacts until the screen lit up with familiarity.

Dad.

His hand hovered over the name. Then he tapped it once and lifted the phone to his ear.

It rang twice before picking up. "Lincoln?" his father's voice came, warm and a little surprised. "Everything alright?"

Lincoln's throat was drier than expected when he answered. "Yeah." It came out too quickly. He cleared his throat and tried again. "Just...wanted to check in. See how the move's coming."

Silence. Then a soft, revealing chuckle. "The move?"

Lincoln shifted. A bird fluttered across the hood, its wings catching flashes of light as it vanished over the awning above the competition doors. "Yeah," he muttered. "I needed a distraction. Thought I'd call and see what box you and mom were arguing about this morning."

His father chuckled again. "Uh-huh. Right. Distraction."

Lincoln said nothing.

Robert didn't hurry. "Your mother is on her fifth round of repacking the same heirloom china. I've been removed from boxing decisions entirely. Apparently, I'm a threat to 'category labeling.'"

Despite himself, Lincoln cracked half a smile. "Sounds like Mom."

Robert added dryly, "She also said if I try to throw out the broken teakettle from our second anniversary, she'll divorce me and take the spoon rest." So I'm staying out of her way.

The familiar cadence of his father's voice—wry as it was—was comforting Lincoln.

"But all the big stuff's done," Robert added. "Movers are confirmed; utilities are set. Pretty soon, it'll all be someone else's house."

That pinched something in Lincoln's chest.

A brief pause lingered between them. Then, softer, Robert asked, "What about your next chapter, huh?"

Lincoln tensed, the small muscles in his forearms pulling tight. "What do you mean?"

Another hum. "Your visit to Serenity wasn't exactly scheduled to last this long. I'd venture that's less about logistics, more about heartburn."

Lincoln's jaw flexed.

His father waited a beat, then, perfectly neutral: "Does this tension, by chance, have anything to do with a Miss Candy Malone?"

Lincoln stared hard at the dashboard. "Can we not?"

Robert chuckled knowingly.

Lincoln sighed. "She's...frustrating."

"Mm." That was all his dad said, but he said it in the tone of someone who had been there.

"What?"

"You were raised by a woman who spirited away your college tuition forms because she didn't like the font," Robert said. "You tell me what that means."

Lincoln went still. His mother wasn't careless or reckless; she simply prioritized happiness, as she always had.

Robert—the steady, practical man who'd married her—had spent years resisting it. Until somewhere along the way, he'd stopped fighting and started choosing it as well. Now, he smiled when she rolled her eyes at him.

Lincoln froze, then chuckled—brief and hesitant.

His father's tone softened, humor giving way to something quieter. "I spent years chasing logic. Believing that if everything was balanced on paper, it would all fall into place. But your mom..." He shook his head; a breath caught on a memory. "She never fit into a plan. She was bright. Loud. Unpredictable. And she never once apologized for it."

The car fell silent around them, and the tick of a cooling engine nearby was the only sound daring to interrupt.

"I almost lost her," Robert continued. "Not because of a big mistake. Just a lot of small ones. Choosing certainty over connection. Efficiency over affection. Trying to control everything meant I controlled nothing that truly mattered."

Lincoln glanced out the windshield. The lobby door across the lot opened, and someone wheeled trays of ingredients into the competition hall. It all looked so orderly. Calm. But for him, everything inside had gone off script days ago.

"Your mother made our lives...brighter," Robert said gently. "But different. Uneven. Harder to forecast."

Lincoln ran a hand through his hair.

"She didn't fit into any of the systems I built," his dad added. "She didn't want to, but she never left. And, thank God, I woke up before I let fear push her out the door." Robert's voice softened even more. "And now I'm hearing my son struggle with something that sounds like..." Another pause. Another chuckle. "Well. Let's call it a familiar kind of chaos."

Lincoln's grip on the steering wheel loosened just a little. He didn't need to ask what his father meant; he already understood.

"Look, son," Robert said. "You've always been good at order. But the thing is, structure doesn't build a life. People do."

That truth settled somewhere deep.

"You called me," his dad said, gentler now. "You already know what you want. You're just waiting for someone to tell you it's okay to want it."

For a moment, all Lincoln could do was breathe.

Then, quietly: "Thanks, Dad."

He could hear the smile in his father's voice. "You're welcome, son. I'm just glad you're smarter than I was and are figuring it out sooner."

The call ended.

Lincoln dropped the phone onto the passenger seat, fingers loosening at last.

He opened the door and walked inside. Into the mess, the unknown, and now he knew exactly what he needed.

The morning light crept across the prep room, shining on the stainless-steel counters. Lincoln saw Candy right away, exactly where he knew she'd be—already at her station. He paused just inside the door and watched.

She hadn't moved since he entered. Her back was straight, but tension coursed through every line of her shoulders. Her cheek rested against her sweater, hands pressed flat on her lap, fingers digging into her thigh. Too still. Too controlled.

Are you really just gonna sit there?

Bailey's voice cut through the quiet—sharp and welcome. Her arms were full with ingredients, tools, or whatever Candy needed, and she moved easily into the space beside her friend. Lincoln felt a flicker of guilt. He should have been there helping, but relief won out because Candy had Bailey, and Bailey was making her fight.

Candy blinked, slow to register, like she was wading back toward herself. When she spoke, her voice was hoarse around the edges. "I—"

"Nope." Bailey raised one hand, cutting her off without apology. "I'm not going to let you spiral. We're not doing that today."

"I'm not spiraling," Candy muttered.

Lincoln kept his expression neutral, but his pulse quickened slightly. There it was again—that steel inside Candice Malone. She didn't want to spiral. She hadn't come this far for that, but she was starting to tip over.

Bailey just glanced at her.

Lincoln observed how Candy's mouth twisted, frustration peeking through her tightly held restraint. "Fine. I'm spiraling a little."

"There it is," Bailey said, crossing her arms with satisfaction.

Lincoln knew better than to insert himself. Not yet. This was Bailey's specialty, and right now Candy didn't need logic. She needed grit.

"Yesterday sucked," Bailey said softly now. "And yeah, he stole from you again. But we're not backing down for him, Candy."

Candy's hands clenched around the edge of the countertop. "And if it's not enough? If I'm not enough?"

Lincoln's throat tightened. There was at least thirty feet between them, and he could still feel the impact of that question hanging in the air like it was personal.

Bailey's face softened. She leaned forward, her fingers wrapping around Candy's wrist. "If you don't fight back, he wins. Tell me, sugar, do you really want to give him that satisfaction?"

A moment passed. Lincoln felt it like a click in the gears—the shift. A low flame behind Candy's eyes flickered, hesitant but still burning.

She exhaled, long and steady. "No."

Bailey smirked. "Absolutely, no."

Lincoln relaxed his fisted hands.

Candy rolled her shoulders back, slowly reclaiming her space. "Now, let's go remind him exactly who he tried to mess with."

The ding of a text buzzed through the air like a live wire. Bailey's fingers quickly moved to her phone at her hip. Her eyes read the message, and all the lightness drained from her face like spilled ink.

Her entire posture sharpened. Jaw locked. Shoulders squared.

Lincoln straightened.

"What?" Candy asked.

Bailey didn't answer.

Lincoln could see the calculation behind her eyes, the tight processing, the moment when damage control turned into something much heavier.

Candy's voice edged tighter. "Bailey."

Bailey looked up. "I need you to sit down."

Candy blinked. "I am sitting."

Lincoln watched the moment unfold from beside them, the air thickening with anticipation. Bailey moved closer, and her voice dropped almost too low for Lincoln to eavesdrop. "Clinton just got back to me. He investigated Bradley's company. The Mulberry Bakery that he entered the contest under."

His stomach twisted. The invisible thread he'd been following for weeks—loose documents, missed payments, that uneasy feeling that something wasn't adding up—tightened into a noose.

Candy nodded once. Tentative. Ready to brace.

Bailey inhaled. "Bradley didn't just steal your recipe, Candy. He used your business credentials to open the second location."

Candy went perfectly still.

Bailey didn't relent. "He listed it all under your EIN, your state license, your insurance forms—"

Candy's head tilted just slightly, not out of confusion but in understanding, as if she didn't want to accept that what was just confirmed was true.

Lincoln swallowed hard. She may not fully understand what this means yet, but he does.

Bailey's voice cooled, sharp as a knife. "He's been using you,

Candy. And now there's proof."

It was like watching a storm cloud gather from within. Candy's breath came through clenched teeth, a low wind under a heavy sky. Her eyes darkened, glassy with fury, but now lined with certainty.

Lincoln saw it click into place, observed the chaos she once managed with jokes turn into something much more dangerous.

Bailey said, "Whatever you're about to do, don't do it here."

Candy's hand twitched, a faint flick of her fingers, restrained. Not fury unleashed; she was taking a note from his book—planning Bradley's downfall. He'd seen CEOs unravel for less.

She locked eyes with Bailey, voice low. "When's the soonest I can take legal action?"

Bailey didn't hesitate. "Clinton's already in motion. We'll have something official by tomorrow."

Lincoln shifted his gaze to the hallway—judges, staff, and competitors murmuring beyond the sliding prep door. He then looked back at Candy just as she straightened herself upright.

"What's the plan, boss?" Bailey asked, but Lincoln had been holding the question in for hours.

Candy leveled her chin, steel running through her spine. "First?" Her voice was calm. *Deadly*. "I win this damn competition."

Bailey's grin was full of mischief. "And then?"

Candy didn't answer immediately. Her gaze flicked past both of them—toward the baking floor beyond the open doors. Toward war. "Then I take back what's mine."

A silence settled.

Lincoln stepped forward, the world narrowing to the space between him and Candy. He uncrossed his arms, watching the storm settle into her expression, and felt a slow burn of pride. "Are we doing this, Malone?"

Her eyes met his. Unflinching. "We are."

Together, they stepped toward the arena.

Bradley didn't realize it yet, but this wasn't Candy at her breaking point. It was her reckoning. And Lincoln would walk into the fire with her, every damn step.

She wasn't just fighting for what had been stolen.

She was taking back what had always been hers.

Chapter Twenty-Eight

Candy

As she stepped onto the competition floor with Lincoln, the world fell away until all she could hear was the steady beat of her heart. The bright studio lights above felt sharper and more focused—like everyone was waiting, watching, and expecting her to slip, but that moment wasn't coming.

He'd surprised her by coming back, but she also knew that's just who he was. Reliable Lincoln beside her, his stride steady, his presence grounding her more than she wanted to admit. After everything, the competition, the sabotage, the fight—they were both still here. Together.

Bailey's words from earlier echoed in Candy's mind.

Bradley didn't just steal your recipe. He stole your business.

It hadn't fully registered, not at first. The depth of what it meant. But now? Now, as she stepped up to her station, it was sinking in.

Bradley had stolen from her in more ways than one. He took her livelihood, used her EIN and business licenses, and damaged her reputation to open a second bakery. While she fought to keep Patty's Cakes afloat, he siphoned off every resource he could, and she was too busy putting out small fires to realize that the whole foundation was already burning.

It had been his plan all along. Once the Mulberry was up and running, Patty's Cakes would no longer be in business, as competition or evidence.

But Candy wasn't distracted anymore.

She adjusted the cuffs of her sleeves and firmly placed her hands on the stainless steel counter. The final challenge was only minutes away. She had a competition to win before dealing with everything outside these walls, and winning was going to be her first move in destroying him.

The host's voice rang out through the loudspeakers, bright and full of manufactured enthusiasm. "Bakers, welcome to the final round of Sweet Success. You've all proven your skills in adaptability and technique, but today?" A dramatic pause. "Today is about more than precision. It's about heart."

Candy exhaled slowly, her fingers twitching as she steadied herself.

"We want each of you to create a signature dessert," the announcer continued. "Something that represents who you are as a baker. This should be a dish that tells a story—the story of your bakery, your passion, and what customers will remember about you."

Another wave of murmurs ran through the competitors. This was the contest's final test. It wasn't just about skill, but about identity.

Candy tightened her apron strings.

She knew exactly who she was, and unlike Bradley, she wasn't pretending or stealing anything from anyone else.

"This is it," Lincoln said. His voice was low, calm, steady.

Candy looked up at him. His sharp gaze wasn't on their workstation but on her, as if he was reading every thought racing through her mind. "Are you ready?" he asked.

She recognized it in the questions; he wasn't asking about the contest, the next two hours, or facing Bradley today.

Lincoln was asking about everything. Was she prepared for what was coming next for them?

Candy's stomach clenched, but the fear she'd carried for weeks faded. She shifted her hips and squared her shoulders. "No," she admitted softly, "but let's do it anyway."

A slow, knowing smile tugged at Lincoln's mouth. Without another word, he picked up the mixing bowl.

They had work to do.

The flour dust swirled under the bright stage lights as Candy worked, her hands moving with confidence and precision. There was no second-guessing today. No hesitating. The lavender-infused batter whipped together beautifully in her hands, blending smoothly with the warmed honey. Beside her, Lincoln measured out the dry ingredients with his usual methodical perfection.

Between them, there was no need for unnecessary conversation. They had done this a dozen times before. But this time?

This time, it wasn't a test recipe; it was *the* recipe. She refused to rush. She refused to let Bradley—or anyone—dictate how she moved, how she baked, how she made magic.

Somewhere in her peripheral vision, she sensed the nervous energy of other contestants. A woman two stations away was frantically icing her multi-layered pastry, while another was still rushing to plate delicate raspberry soufflés.

Candy carefully placed each lavender-honey patty cake onto its ceramic dish, dusting it lightly with powdered sugar and adding a delicate curl of candied lemon.

Energy crackled in the air around her, while every contestant hurried to craft their own signature piece. A contestant to her left hurried to fire a decadent crème brûlée, while another furiously piped chocolate accents onto an extravagant, towering confection. Their nerves filled the air, but Candy blocked it all out.

She had one focus, and that was making sure Bradley never forgot this loss.

"Last call," the announcer's voice rang through the room. "Three minutes remaining!"

Candy and Lincoln moved perfectly in sync. The lavender-honey-infused Patty Cake sat proudly on their ceramic plates, its golden top glistening under the competition lights.

A hush settled over the kitchen.

It was time.

The judges approached.

The silver-haired judge, the one Candy had unintentionally

started watching for approval, was the first to reach for a plate. She examined the cake. "Tell us about this dish."

"It's a variation of my mother's original Patty Cake recipe." Candy exhaled, steadying herself. "But it's not hers. It's mine."

Silence. The judge watched her, listening for more.

Candy pressed on, her voice calm and steady. "Lavender for a touch of something unexpected—the thing you don't expect to fall in love with, but once you do, you'll never forget it." Her eyes flickered toward Lincoln, just for a moment, before she looked back at the judges. "Honey for warmth, nostalgia, and the sweetness in every shared kitchen across generations." She took a small breath. "And lemon zest to cut through—the reminder that love, like life, should always have a little edge."

The moment lingered just long enough for Candy's breath to catch.

Then, the lead judge took a slow bite.

A small, knowing smile curled on the judge's lips. "The floral balance is delicate," she murmured. "The honey is perfect, and the citrus?" She glanced up, eyes sharp with something close to admiration. "The perfect counterbalance. A reminder that sweetness is best when met with a little boldness."

Candy's pulse stuttered.

Another judge took a bite. Nodded. "You've taken something simple and made it unforgettable."

And then the last judge leaned back with a grin, tapping his fork against the dish. "It doesn't just taste good. It feels good, too."

Candy barely heard them.

All she could hear was her own heartbeat slamming against

her ribs.

This. This was *her* Patty Cake.

The judge put his fork down. "It's a cake that tells a story," he said with a nod. "And it's a pretty darn good one."

Candy barely heard the words as the rankings flashed across the screen.

1st Place: Candy Malone – Lavender-Honey Patty Cakes

2nd Place: Bradley Tanner – Mulberry Cake

3rd Place: Jenna Michaels – Raspberry Souffle

And just like that—it was *over.*

She had won.

They had won.

Candy glanced at Lincoln, ready to scream or celebrate, but before she could move, she caught a glimpse from the corner of her eye.

Across the room, Sabrina entered the contest kitchen and walked straight toward the judges.

Candy's pulse kicked up for a different reason entirely.

Something inside her said, *"watch this."*

The woman didn't hesitate. She stepped forward holding a familiar, thick binder, and quietly placed it on the judges' table.

The head judge frowned. "What's this?"

Sabrina set her jaw. "Proof that his business, the one he entered under," she said, stabbing a finger toward Bradley without sparing him a glance. "It was never his at all."

Silence crashed over the room.

Candy did not move.

She barely breathed.

From the corner of her vision, she saw Bradley, frozen mid-smirk. Then, just as quickly, he laughed as if it was all a misunderstanding. "Sabrina, what the hell are you doing?"

She turned to face him fully for the first time.

And Candy? Oh, she lived for the fire flashing behind that woman's eyes.

"Something I should have done a long time ago." Bradley opened his mouth, but Sabrina steamrolled ahead, thoroughly and completely done. "He stole her business." She pointed straight at Candy. "Used her licensing, her financial records. That bakery he entered under? It's still under her damn name."

A gasp rippled through the crowd.

Candy inhaled sharply—feeling all that rage, exhaustion, and the constant struggle just to breathe crushing down on her at once. But she didn't stop or say anything because she knew she didn't need to. Sabrina had taken care of it.

She lifted her chin. Candy didn't even have to say "I told you so," because Bradley, the man who had always been smooth, quick, and skilled at worming his way out of trouble—had nothing left to say.

Chapter Twenty-Nine

Candy

The competition hall had gone quiet. At the judges' table, a thick binder lay open, documents spilling across the white cloth. The lead judge flipped through page after page, her expression sharpening with each turn.

Bradley recovered quickly, slipping into his familiar charm. "What's this about?" he asked, chuckling softly. "Some kind of misunderstanding?"

"Not a misunderstanding," Sabrina said, stepping forward, her voice firm. "A correction."

Candy's breath caught.

Bradley tilted his head. "Maybe you should explain what you're accusing me of before you cause unnecessary drama."

Sabrina's laugh was humorless. "Unnecessary? Imagine my surprise when I dug into our business filings and realized every supplier account, every license, and every financial record for The Mulberry Café still lists Patty's Cakes. Legally, this was never your bakery, Bradley. It was hers. Even that stupid binder belongs to her! You've been using Ms. Patty's old recipes."

Gasps rippled through the room as the judges exchanged glances, and murmurs spread like wildfire.

Sabrina didn't stop. "You didn't build a business. You stole one. Using Candy's name, her paperwork, her legacy. And worse—you let me believe it was ours."

Bradley's jaw clenched, but the tension was visible. His grin remained fixed, edges starting to fray. "That's ridiculous. Maybe a clerical error—"

"You forged signatures," Sabrina snapped, thrusting a document toward the judges. "I don't even know why you're here and not in jail."

The judges leaned over the file, whispers turning into outrage.

Candy's pulse thundered. For the first time, people saw Bradley exactly for who he truly was.

The lead judge straightened. "We'll need to review this immediately."

They huddled together, clucking and waving their arms. After a few minutes, the head judge left the group and picked up the microphone on the judge's table. "Hello, everyone, thank you for your patience. We're standing by our decision. Ms. Malone, representing Patty's Cakes, will be taking home our first-place prize. We will review our notes and confirm the second and third-place winners, which will be announced tomorrow. Mr. Tanner has been disqualified from the competition.

Candy exhaled, adrenaline finally breaking through months of fear and exhaustion. Relief settled heavy but genuine.

Bailey moved next to her, phone in hand. "Clinton's already handling the legal side. His lawyers will want to speak soon. We'll need to retrieve that binder from the judges."

Bradley's expression darkened. "You think this is the end?"

Candy met his eyes, her voice steady. "No. I know it is."

The head organizer stepped forward, voice firm. "Mr. Tanner, you need to come with us."

Bradley clenched his fists, but for once, he didn't have an out. He didn't even try. He was escorted off the floor, his hollow grin finally gone.

Bailey gave Candy's arm a squeeze. "You just handed your ex his downfall on a silver platter. Try to at least look like you're enjoying this."

A shaky laugh escaped her, light and breathless.

Bailey's smirk softened as her gaze flicked toward Lincoln. "And on that note, I'll leave you to more important things." With a wink, she melted into the crowd.

Candy turned, and there he was. Lincoln. Still at her side. Still watching her.

Something inside her shifted.

He slid his hands into his pockets. "Looks like you got what you wanted."

She swallowed, throat tight. He wasn't just talking about Bradley. "Yeah."

He studied her, eyes unreadable but intent. "So, what happens now?"

That question rooted her in place. He could still leave. She could still let him. The safe thing would be to step back, let him go back to New York and his structure, his logic.

But she wasn't afraid anymore. Candy inhaled and said, "I think...no. I know. I don't want you to go."

Something shifted in him, sharp and visible, like the ground moving beneath them. His lips parted, surprised.

She smiled nervously. "Only if you want to stay, of course—"

Lincoln kissed her. No hesitation. No second-guessing.

His hands framed her face, warm and steady, as if he already done the math and this—her—was the only solution that ever made sense. Candy curled her fingers into his shirt, anchoring herself to the moment.

When he pulled away, his forehead rested against hers, a crooked grin tugging at his lips. "You talked too much before letting me do that."

"I had to be sure."

His gaze softened. "And are you?"

Her smile spread, steady now. She brushed her nose against his, heart racing in the best possible way. "Completely."

Chapter Thirty

Candy

Outside the assisted living facility entrance, Candy cradled the bakery box in her hands, the warm scent of freshly baked treats drifting up to meet her. The late afternoon sun dipped low in the sky, casting a gentle golden light over the brick pathways and flower beds. The sharp scent of freshly cut grass mixed with the distant hum of laughter coming from an open window in the common room.

She had walked through these doors many times before, but today felt different. Today, she carried more than just pastries.

It was over—the competition, the mess with Bradley. She had fought, she had won, and now there was one more person she wanted to share this with.

Taking a steady breath, she stepped inside, the familiar hum of low conversation and distant piano music filling her ears. As she moved down the hall, her pulse kept an irregular rhythm. She wasn't sure whether today would be good or bad, but she had promised herself that, no matter what, she would be here to see her mom.

Patricia Brinley sat in her bedroom, in her favorite chair by the window, wrapped in a thin afghan despite the summer heat. She gazed out at the garden with her hands neatly folded in her lap.

Candy hesitated for just a second before softly knocking on the doorframe. "Hey, Mama."

Her mother turned slowly, blinking as if she needed a moment to recognize the voice. But then, understanding appeared on her face, and a gentle, soft smile followed. "My sweet girl," she murmured.

Candy swallowed hard against the tightness in her throat and stepped forward, perching herself on the chair beside her mother. "I brought you something." She lifted the bakery box, setting it gently on the small table between them before carefully opening the lid.

Inside, five perfectly baked lavender-honey Patty Cakes sat neatly in rows, glazed with her lavender citrus coating.

Her mother's gaze stayed on them for a long moment, appreciating the familiar shape and careful craftsmanship. Then she reached out with delicate fingers, taking one into her hands.

The moment was fragile. Candy had no idea if she even remembered what these cakes stood for. Slowly, her mother took a bite, and Candy didn't breathe.

For several seconds, Patricia chewed thoughtfully, a small hum vibrating in the back of her throat. Then, her eyes fluttered open, a flicker of recognition passing through them.

"Mmm..." She took another slow bite, savoring it. Her gaze drifted toward Candy, a warm and knowing expression settling on her face. "You changed it."

Candy's breath caught. "Just a little."

Patricia smiled—soft, approving. "Lavender," she murmured, voice laced with quiet recognition. "Not just mama's Patty Cake anymore."

Candy swallowed hard and said, "No," she admitted, her voice barely above a whisper. "It's mine now."

Patricia nodded, still smiling as she reached out and lightly patted Candy's hand. "Good," she said softly. "That's how it should be."

She hadn't expected permission — not in words, at least — but here it was. A moment of clarity, a final thread tying the past and the future together.

Then, her mother's gaze drifted past Candy, gazing into the distance as if she could see through walls and beyond time itself. She offered her a knowing smile.

"You didn't do this alone, did you, sugar?" Patricia murmured, her voice gentle but confident.

Candy swallowed past the lump in her throat. "No, Mama. I didn't."

Her mother nodded slightly, as if this was the answer she had expected. "That's good," she said, settling back into her chair. "You'll need love to carry you through. Family. Friends. The right kind of people standing beside you."

Candy squeezed her mother's hand, her throat tightening. "I've got them."

Patricia let out a quiet laugh, nodding her head. "I wasn't always the best at choosing men," she admitted, her gaze turning thoughtful. "But I always had good friends, and I had you." She gently patted Candy's hand; her fingers were cool but steady. "And you? You won't be alone either."

Candy pressed her lips together, trying to keep her emotions in check.

Patricia's eyes were hazy but warm, filled with a sense of peace—like knowing. Her mother took another slow bite of the patty cake, her expression softening. "It tastes like home," she murmured.

Candy inhaled deeply, her fingers tightening slightly around her mother's.

"Yeah," she whispered, her voice thick. "It does."

Patricia smiled again, her eyelids growing heavy. She tilted her head slightly to the side, her breathing evening out. "Your daddy always said a recipe ain't just flour and sugar," she mused, her words slipping into the quiet between them. "He got one thing right. It's love. Passed down. Given freely."

Candy blinked rapidly, her vision blurring.

Her mother sighed, a content sound, her grip still resting loosely over Candy's hand.

She gritted her teeth, her throat too thick for words. There were so many things she wanted to say—how she had been fighting to keep the bakery afloat, about Bradley and everything he had stolen, and how she had almost lost herself in the process—about how much harder it had been doing all of it alone. But instead, she reached out, carefully smoothing a stray curl from her mother's forehead. "I won, Mama," she whispered. "Sweet Success. I did it."

Her mother made a gentle sound of approval, nodding as she absentmindedly broke off another small piece of cake. "I knew you would."

Candy exhaled, her shoulders shaking just a little.

Not long after, her mother's eyes grew heavier, her movements slowed, and it wasn't long before her breathing softened into sleep. Candy stayed beside her, watching the gentle rise and fall of her mother's chest, memorizing the soft sound of peace.

After all the chaos, fights, and uncertainty, this was where she needed to be most.

Carefully, she leaned in and pressed a light kiss to her mother's temple. "I'm going to take care of Patty's Cakes," she whispered. "I promise."

With that, she grabbed the bakery box, gave her mother one last look, and then stepped back toward the door.

She didn't know how much longer she had with her. But today?

Today had been a good day. A really good day.

Chapter Thirty-One

Lincoln

Most of the packing was done.

Lincoln stood outside his parents' house, hands in his pockets, looking at the moving truck in the driveway. The furniture was wrapped, the boxes labeled, and soon his parents would officially leave Serenity behind.

And if he stuck to his original plan, so would he.

A sharp breeze swept through the late afternoon air, rustling the trees along the quiet street. He should be inside, helping with the last of the packing. Instead, he stood there, unmoving, watching the house that had once been his home fade into a place that no longer belonged to him.

Footsteps scraped against the pavement behind him.

Lincoln exhaled. He didn't need to turn around to know who it was.

"I thought you'd be gone by now," Robert Grant said, his voice steady as he came to stand beside his son. He wasn't holding a box or a clipboard, just two steaming mugs of coffee.

Lincoln accepted the offered cup silently.

His father leaned against the car, exhaling as he looked at the house. "Your mother cried six times today."

Lincoln snorted. "That's less than I expected."

Robert let out a quiet laugh, shaking his head before taking a slow sip of his coffee. Then, after a moment, he added, "And you? Why are you still here?"

Lincoln stiffened. "Still packing."

Robert made a sound in the back of his throat, somewhere between a hum and a knowing chuckle. "Sure."

Lincoln exhaled slowly, gripping the coffee cup a bit tighter than needed. He could feel his father's gaze on him—patient, waiting. Not pushing, not forcing anything out of him.

Just waiting.

Then, after a long moment, his father simply said, "It's Candy, isn't it?"

Lincoln closed his eyes briefly. Of course, his father knew.

Robert didn't press right away; he just let the silence stretch before tipping his cup toward the house. "You know, I spent so much of my life thinking I had time to focus on what mattered later. Thought as long as I took care of the numbers, provided, and built everything in neat little boxes, it would add up." He let out a quiet, reflective chuckle. "Then, one day, your mother told me she was done waiting for me to live in the life we were building."

Lincoln frowned. "You were already living it."

Robert turned, meeting his son's gaze. "I was managing it."

Something inside Lincoln tightened.

His father studied him before tipping his head slightly.

"You have to ask yourself something, Son—are you managing your life, or are you actually living it?"

Lincoln hadn't told his dad about the fight with Candy or the words they exchanged. He didn't need to because Robert already knew. He always did.

Lincoln exhaled. "I know she's something special, and I know we fit together. We add up. But, Dad, she's not leaving here. I can want her, and she can want me, but the question is, do I want Serenity?"

"It was your home, once."

"She has roots here, deep ones. Her business, her friends, and her mother."

"Well, and we're moving away."

There's that, too," Lincoln said, looking at his dad to gauge his reaction before asking, "I'd need to make Serenity my home, just as my home is rolling away in the back of an eighteen-wheeler."

You can't think about us, and you know that. We'll come back for visits, and who knows what your momma will want in a few years. I'm not sure I could keep her away from Serenity if she had grand babies here.

"Whoa, we can slow down that freight train." He took a long sip of his coffee and said, "Dad, I don't know what she wants."

Robert chuckled. "Son..." He clapped a firm hand on Lincoln's shoulder. "You're a numbers man. Smart. Calculated. But, you ain't got no sense when it comes to a woman like her." He shook his head, fondness weaving into his voice. "It's not about knowing. Lord knows, she'll keep you on your toes for the rest of your life. It's about choosing. Half the time you won't know what you're doing, but that's what you're choosing."

Lincoln inhaled sharply, something setting straight in his chest.

Robert gave his son's shoulder a final squeeze before stepping back. "Now," he said, turning toward the house, "I'm going inside before your mother decides to change her mind and make me unpack all these boxes. But you?" He made a shooing motion with his hand, smirking. "You have somewhere else to be."

Lincoln watched him disappear inside.

Then, after one long, grounding breath, he started the car.

Chapter Thirty-Two

Candy

With slow, deliberate strokes Candy wiped down the bakery counter dragging the damp towel over the stainless-steel surface for far longer than necessary. The stray flour dust had already been cleared, the last batch of pastries for the day safely packed away—but she couldn't bring herself to stop.

Because if she stopped, she had to think, and thinking meant acknowledging the one thing she still hadn't finished.

Lincoln.

The bell above the bakery door jingled.

Candy turned.

As if she'd summoned him with her thoughts, he stood in the doorway—hands in his pockets, shoulders back, his stare fixed on hers.

Her grip tightened around the dish towel. For a few stretched seconds, she paused. "You're still here," she murmured.

Lincoln exhaled softly, an unreadable flicker passing across his face. "Still here."

Candy could tell he wasn't here because he'd changed his mind or because he'd decided on anything. This was a goodbye.

She could stop him. Maybe with the right words, she could take the leap, throw herself into something uncertain and un-scripted. To be fair, that's how she'd always handled things. Instead, she set the towel down. "We, uh...never really talked about this, did we?" Her voice was quieter than she meant it to be, but she didn't correct it.

Lincoln tilted his head slightly. "About what happens now?" His voice was just as soft.

"Right." Candy nodded, lips pressing together. "We know we have *us*, but we never figured out how to make that work *here*."

Lincoln inhaled, weighing his words carefully—perhaps too carefully, as if calculating the odds before even trying to play his hand.

Candy beat him to it.

"I don't want to pressure you into a big decision," she said quickly, then let out a small, almost frustrated laugh. "I mean, this whole thing wasn't supposed to be like this."

Lincoln studied her for a beat. "And yet here we are."

"Yep. Here we are." She let out a slow exhale.

"I don't like not having a plan."

"Yeah," she whispered, her throat tight. "I figured."

Another small, almost reluctant smirk tugged at the corner of his mouth. "You don't do plans."

Candy shrugged, unsure if it was amusement or regret weighing her chest. "I'm trying."

Lincoln's gaze caught hers, and just for a second—just one second—she let herself wonder what would happen if she asked him to stay. If she just took the leap, but she didn't.

They hadn't thought this far ahead. They had spent weeks pushing toward something, but now that the goal was behind them, they were left hanging, uncertain if—or where—they should land.

Lincoln sighed and looked past her at the bakery's warm, familiar space. "I don't even know what I'd do here," he admitted.

Candy tried to keep her voice light. "Oh, I don't know. Crunch numbers, scare off incompetent suppliers, argue with me about ingredient costs."

Lincoln let out a quiet laugh. "Tempting."

Candy swallowed. "But not enough?"

His lips pressed together. "I like structure."

"And I like mess."

"I noticed." Lincoln's half-smile was soft.

Candy sighed. "That's the problem, isn't it?"

Lincoln hesitated, then answered honestly. "Maybe."

Her chest ached, but she nodded, willing herself to accept it.

They were still Candy and Lincoln. Still a woman who thrived on instinct and a man who only moved forward when everything was calculated and controlled, and they didn't know if those two things could fit together outside of a bakery crisis.

Candy took a slow breath. "We can...keep in touch?" The words felt unnatural coming out of her mouth, too measured, too cautious for someone like her.

Lincoln nodded once. "Yeah. We should."

Candy tried for a forced smile. "Make an actual plan."

Lincoln looked at her—half amused, and half something else. "Who are you, and what have you done with Candy Malone?"

Candy snorted. "I knew you'd say something."

His lips twitched. "Classic me."

Candy exhaled, watching as his gaze flickered toward the door.

This was it.

The choice they weren't fully ready to make.

"I should go," Lincoln said softly.

Candy nodded, even though it felt wrong. "Okay."

Lincoln held her gaze for a moment longer, his jaw tightening slightly—like he should say something else, but didn't have the words.

He reached for the doorknob.

Her stomach twisted.

He paused.

And without turning, he said, "This...doesn't feel finished."

Candy let out a breath she hadn't realized she was holding. "No," she admitted. "It doesn't."

A beat.

Then, just barely, he nodded.

And then—he walked out the door. She resisted the urge to chase and to jump.

Instead, she let herself wait and watched the door close behind him.

The neon glow of The Wagon Wheel flickered in the warm Texas evening, casting a familiar golden hue over the line of trucks parked outside the bar. Candy stepped out of Bailey's car, senses filled with the smells of fried chicken and whiskey.

Tonight was supposed to be a celebration—a way for Bailey, Taylor, and Molly to pull her out of her head and remind her that she had won. The financial battle she'd been fighting for months had finally ended in her favor. Bradley was done. Patty's Cakes was hers again, but Candy sort of hated how the story was ending.

"Sugar, if you look this stressed at the start of girls' night, I'm going to be forced to order you a double," Bailey mused, looping her arm through Candy's and tugging her toward the entrance.

Candy huffed. "I'm fine."

"Honeybee," Taylor drawled, side-eyeing her as they walked, "your face is doing this thing where it looks like you swallowed a lemon whole."

Molly, the designated driver for the evening, let out a conspiratorial hum. "Is this about Lincoln?"

Candy stumbled slightly on the doorstep. "What?"

Bailey and Taylor groaned in unison.

"Was I not supposed to say anything?" Molly's boots crunched on the loose gravel as she abruptly stopped. "I'm sorry, Taylor didn't say. Bailey! Why didn't you tell me?"

"We needed girl time. You've been holed up getting everything ready for this new baby. It's been too long!" Bailey said as she tugged the door open. A wave of country music and laughter spilled out, washing over them with the scent of smoky barbecue and warm beer. "Finally."

Candy pulled a face. "Finally, what?"

Taylor smirked, flipping her blond waves over her shoulder as they walked inside. "Finally, we can stop pretending we don't know what—or who—has you all twisted up inside your pretty little head."

Candy opened her mouth to argue, but Molly was already snickering behind her, tapping her belly as she led them toward a booth near the back. "Not to sound selfish, but I love that I get to be sober for this."

"Oh, you love the mess," Bailey teased, signaling a bartender.

"I live for it." Molly slid into the booth, placing a protective hand over her stomach as she got comfortable. "Best entertainment around."

Candy sighed, rubbing her eyes. "I'm not twisted up about Lincoln."

Bailey merely raised an eyebrow. "Really?"

"Nope. Not at all." Candy grabbed a peanut from the bowl on the table and popped it into her mouth. "We had a mature discussion. We said we'd keep talking. I'm totally fine."

Taylor toyed with the rim of her margarita glass. "Uh-huh. That's why you've avoided saying his name all night."

Molly leaned forward, resting her arms on the table. "Ohh, you *like* like him, don't you?"

Silence.

Candy rolled an unshelled peanut between her fingers, feeling the urge to disappear. "That's not the problem."

Bailey sighed and leaned forward. "Alright, then, what is the problem?"

Candy exhaled slowly, gazing at her drink. "I don't trust it."

The table went silent for the first time all evening.

Bailey rested her chin on her hand, her eyes softening. "Why?"

Candy swallowed, fingers tightening around the glass. "Because...what if it's just the mess? What if it's just right now?" She picked at the condensation on the glass. "We've been caught up in deadlines, stress, the competition. What if, when it all settles, we realize it never should've been anything more? We're total opposites."

Bailey let out a long-suffering sigh. "Candy, I hate to break it to you, but that man sticks around when things are hard. You think he's suddenly going to dip when life gets easier?"

Candy swallowed.

Molly shook her head, grinning as she rested her chin in her hand. "This is adorable. She thinks she has a choice in the matter."

Taylor smirked, nudging Candy's knee under the table. "My favorite part is how she doesn't even realize she's already in love with him."

Candy almost choked on air. "Excuse me?"

"Oh, honey..." Bailey sipped her margarita for dramatic effect. "You're already gone for this man."

Candy let out a very unconvincing laugh. "I am not in love with Lincoln. I just really like when we're naked."

Taylor raised a finger. "Then why do you care so much about whether it's real?"

Candy shut her mouth.

Bailey's smirk deepened. "There it is."

Molly nodded, sipping her lemon water. "Wow. That was quick."

Candy groaned, covering her face.

Bailey nudged her foot under the table. "Sugar, he's in love with you, too."

Candy swallowed hard.

Seeming to sense the change in her energy, Taylor leaned forward, tilting her head. "You already know that, don't you?"

Candy didn't have an actual answer for that, but she *felt* it.

In the way he never left her side, in the way he matched her chaos with logic, steadied her hands when she doubted herself. And maybe, in the way he looked at her, as if he wasn't sure if she was ever real until now.

Molly put down her drink, sighing. "Well, there's only one logical thing to do."

Candy lifted a brow. "What's that?"

Molly grinned.

Taylor smirked.

"You gotta go get your man. We need a plan!" Bailey beamed as she flagged down a passing waitress. "We're gonna need another round."

Candy fumbled with her phone, squinting at the screen as the car jerked wildly around a corner.

"Oh my god, Bailey, where did you even learn to drive?" she yelped, clutching the door handle as her screen blurred from motion and maybe also tequila.

"I didn't!" Bailey announced proudly from the back seat. "That's why Molly's driving!"

From the front, Molly—calm, sober, and completely worn out from the chaos behind her—held the wheel with the tired patience of someone who has long understood she's the only thing preventing disaster and a car full of drunk idiots on a mission.

"Might I remind y'all," Molly said in a slow, deliberate Texas drawl, "that I am growing a child inside of me, and I will not be letting this car crash because the three of you can't contain your dramatic love-struck selves while I'm stuck playing taxi."

Candy waved a hand dismissively, trying—and failing—to type a coherent text to Lincoln.

Candy: Incoming. Stop being so hot ablut everything.
Candy: About.
Candy: I men ablut.
Candy: man
Lincoln: ...do I need to call emergency services or just meet you at the hotel door?

Taylor leaned over her shoulder from behind, reading the texts aloud. "God, watching you text is like watching a toddler go after a Google search bar with fists."

Candy elbowed her away. "It's getting the job done."

"Oh, I bet it is," Taylor quipped, kicking her boots up on the passenger seat. "Any chance you're going to actually use words when you see him, or are you just gonna throw yourself at him with big reckless feelings and hope for the best?"

Candy scoffed, accidentally dropping her phone on the floor. "I am not reckless."

Bailey wheezed so hard she started coughing.

Even Molly snorted.

Candy sat up indignantly. "I'M NOT."

Molly kept her eyes firmly on the road, her hands gripping the wheel tighter as she narrowly avoided rear-ending a pickup truck. "Mm-hmm. It's really convincing when you say that while hurtling toward a man's hotel at full speed with no plan beyond 'be attractive and yell.'"

Bailey leaned forward, her eyes gleaming with delight. "Listen, the only thing Candy does better than baking is dramatic declarations. I mean, there was that time in tenth grade when she told Kent Erington I liked him. People still talk about her apology at the fall talent show. I say we let her do her thing."

Taylor raised her to-go margarita cup, clearly smuggled from the bar, and nodded. "Remember: Big feelings. Minimal dignity."

Candy grinned. "Both are my love language."

Molly exhaled sharply, lifting one hand in a threatening but motherly waggle. "Y'all better keep your drunk bits IN THIS CAR, because I swear to biscuits and baby Jesus, if any of you fall out while I'm parking, I will turn this car around, install a car seat, and strap your whiskey asses inside."

"Molly's gonna make a great mom," Bailey mused. "Honestly, it wouldn't even be the weirdest way I've been forced to sober up,"

Taylor looked thoroughly impressed. "I want that story later."

"Me, too." Bailey nodded. "Molly, you countried up real fast."

"Maybe y'all are driving me to it."

"No, you're driving us!" Taylor winked and toasted the air with her nearly empty straw cup. "To hot accountants and questionable rescue plans."

"Cheers," Bailey agreed.

Candy grabbed her phone off the floor, double-checking that Lincoln had responded.

Lincoln: Since I can hear screeching in the distance, I'm going to assume you're close?

Candy grinned.

Candy: Two minutes. Don't move.

Bailey squealed. "Oh my god, YOU'RE REALLY DOING THIS."

Candy pounded on the roof of the car in excitement. "WE ARE REALLY DOING THIS."

Molly gripped the wheel even tighter. "We are really going to kill all of us if you don't let me DRIVE."

Taylor leaned forward, adjusting Candy's top like a stern but supportive auntie. "Alright, lovebird, deep breaths. This is a smart decision made by drunk women with impeccable instincts."

Candy nodded fervently. "Yeah. And the instincts say—"

Molly slammed the brakes outside the hotel.

"You better not puke in my car," she warned, throwing the gear into park.

Candy jumped out of the car before anyone could stop her. *Big feelings. Minimal dignity.*

She ran toward the hotel entrance, catching sight of Lincoln just as he stepped out of the lobby—his arms crossed, his expression an equal mix of amusement and pure exasperated affection.

She skidded to a stop in front of him, breathless, flushed, and completely still, and a little drunk.

His gaze flickered over her rapidly, assessing. "You good?"

Candy, without hesitation, grabbed him by the shirt collar and kissed him so passionately he might have actually missed a category three hurricane if one had blown by.

Bailey, Taylor, and Molly all screamed in delight from the car.

Lincoln kissed her right back.

Chapter Thirty-Three

Candy

The hotel lobby door swished shut behind them, blocking out the distant, drunken cheers from Bailey, Taylor, and Molly, who were still half-hanging out of the car. Candy barely noticed them now. She hardly noticed anything except Lincoln, his hands still gripping her waist, his chest rising and falling as he stared down at her, breathless and stunned.

She had kissed him.

Correction: She had stormed into his life—again—grabbed him by his very well-pressed shirt, and kissed the logic out of him, and he'd kissed her right back.

Lincoln rubbed a hand over his face, his lips twitching as he exhaled—half amusement, half overwhelmed bafflement. "Are you going to explain what just happened, or should I just assume you were kidnapped by a group of drunk beauty pageant moms and dumped here as part of some elaborate scheme to get me to reassess my phone plan?"

Candy grinned, unapologetic. "A little bit of both."

Lincoln huffed out a laugh, shaking his head as he studied her. "You smell like margaritas."

"I was peer-pressured into girls' night." She poked his chest. "But that's not the important part."

"Oh?" Lincoln arched a knowing brow. "And the important part would be?"

Her smile softened into something more certain. With a steady breath, she stepped closer—not dramatic this time, not frantic—but purposeful. She flattened her palms over the soft cotton of his shirt. "That I don't want you to leave."

Lincoln stilled.

No twitch of the mouth, no teasing smirk. Just quiet, careful silence.

Candy swallowed. "I don't know what this looks like, yet. Sure, you'll have to leave, but I want you to come back. I don't have any grand plan. Which, frankly, you should be used to by now."

The corner of his mouth almost lifted at that.

But I do know, she continued, her voice softening, that things haven't felt right since you walked out of the bakery door.

Lincoln clenched his jaw, exhaling through his nose. "Candy—"

"And I know you don't do messy," she interrupted gently, pressing her fingers a little firmer against his chest. "I know you don't like making decisions without analyzing every possible outcome. But maybe—just this once—you decide what feels right instead of what makes sense."

Lincoln's throat bobbed as he swallowed. He didn't answer immediately. Instead, he exhaled slowly, as if he was steadying himself.

Then, carefully, he reached up, sliding his fingers along her jaw and tilting her chin slightly until her eyes locked onto his.

We make sense. I wasn't leaving for me," he admitted, voice quiet but heavy. "I was leaving because I thought that's what you wanted.

Candy's breath hitched.

He studied her face, his thumb barely brushing her cheek. "And I was ready to go. I was." He shook his head, a soft laugh escaping. "But somehow, every road, every mile, every logical reason kept leading me back here to you."

Candy's throat tightened. "So, what happens now?"

"I stay." Lincoln exhaled sharply. "Well, to be specific, I leave, get my things in order, and come back, but then I stay."

A surge of emotion so intense it almost knocked her legs out from under her swept through her chest. "Yeah?"

Lincoln's slow, lopsided smirk finally returned. "Yeah."

Candy grinned, grabbing the front of his shirt. "Good." Then she kissed him, and as she pulled back, her eyes sparkling with something playful, full of light, she whispered against his mouth, "Took you long enough."

Lincoln huffed. "For the record, I want it noted that your dramatic cowboy-movie charge into this hotel is what forced my hand."

"You love dramatics."

Lincoln exhaled through his nose, smirking. "I'm learning to tolerate them."

Candy grinned. "That's basically the same thing."

His arms tightened around her waist, pulling her closer.

"Mm. Jury's still out."

Better settle in, then," she murmured.

Lincoln kissed her again, sealing both their fates, and neither of them held back.

Epilogue

Candy & Lincoln

The aroma of warm vanilla and sugared lavender filled the air, swirling through Patty's Cakes' cozy kitchen as Candy spread the final glaze over a fresh batch of pastries. The afternoon sunlight poured through the small kitchen window.

She paused, absorbing the scene. The bakery belonged to her, and it was doing well.

The past few weeks had been hectic, dealing with the legalities and final arrangements of reclaiming everything Bradley had taken, registering the second location under her own name, updating suppliers, and reassuring their most loyal customers that yes, Patty's Cakes was here to stay. Through it all, Lincoln had stayed too.

That part still startles her sometimes. She'd wake up, half-expecting him to be gone, half-expecting herself to retreat before feelings got too tangled. But every morning? He was still there. Not just existing within her world but choosing to be in it.

A pair of warm, steady arms wrapped around her waist, pulling her back against a firm chest.

"Didn't even flinch," Lincoln murmured against her ear. "I must be losing my touch."

Candy smirked, leaning into him. "You're predictable."

"I prefer efficient," he corrected, his chin resting on her shoulder. "I finished painting the master bedroom at my parent's—my house."

"Hard to adjust?"

"Yes, and no." Lincoln pulled her closer. "If I'm staying here, I want a home. It made sense. I couldn't stay in the hotel forever."

"I'm glad you decided to keep the house." Candy took a step back and studied his face.

"What's got that look on your face?"

She arched a brow. "What look?"

The 'I'm contemplating something deeply sentimental but refusing to admit it' look.

Candy sighed, tilting her head against his. "I was just...appreciating a moment."

Lincoln hummed, pressing a slow, deliberate kiss to the curve of her neck. "Should I leave you and the moment alone?"

Candy snorted, turning in his arms. "Don't you dare."

His eyes sparkled with quiet amusement as he studied her face, fingers tracing slow circles on her lower back. A faint dusting of powdered sugar shadowed his forearm, evidence that he had been sneaking tastes from the pastry case again.

Candy smirked. "You know, for someone who tried to pretend he wasn't into baking, you sure spend a lot of time in my kitchen."

Lincoln seemed completely unbothered. "Our kitchen."

Candy's breath hitched. Not just because of the phrase itself, but the way he said it. Like it was permanent.

She tilted her chin, playing it off with a quirk of her lips. "Oh? And who decided that?"

Lincoln's hands slid lower, his touch teasing along the small of her back. "I believe we did."

Candy was not completely immune to the way he looked at her. "Mm. You really are getting good at this."

"I'm an enthusiastic learner." Lincoln's smirk returned.

Candy grinned. "Dangerous."

"For you? Always."

She barely had time to roll her eyes before the front door slammed open, and the familiar jingle of the bell was almost drowned out by the sheer force of Bailey's entrance.

"I knew it!" Bailey declared loudly, hands on her hips. "I knew you two were in here being disgustingly cute."

Candy groaned, pulling away from Lincoln as Bailey tossed her bag down. "That could mean so many things," Candy muttered.

Bailey waved a hand. "Relax, hun. I know better than to interrupt his meticulous groping."

Lincoln choked on a laugh, while Candy just tossed a towel at Bailey's head.

Bailey caught it easily and plopped onto a stool, grinning. "So, Mr. Numbers, how does it feel being an official partner of Patty's Cakes?"

Lincoln slid onto the stool next to Candy, casually reaching for a cookie. "Tolerable."

Candy smacked his hand away. "Excuse me?"

Bailey cackled. "See, now I get why you like him. He's just as insufferable as you are."

Taylor sauntered in next, eyes shining at the clear change between Candy and Lincoln. "Oh, good, lovebirds and sugar. My two favorite things."

Bailey leaned her chin on her hand. "Dibs on being maid of honor when this eventually turns into wedding cakes instead of Patty Cakes."

"You have to stop." Candy groaned.

"I won't," Bailey corrected gleefully. "And neither will Serenity. Everyone knows what's going on here."

Candy narrowed her eyes. "What's going on here is that I run a bakery, and I have a new partner. Thank you very much."

Molly, who had slipped in quietly, gave a knowing little nod. "Mm-hmm, and he's a lot better than the old one you had."

"Wouldn't take much," Lincoln said flatly. "I'm here for administrative structure."

Everyone stared at him.

He sighed, surrendering. "And Candy."

Bailey cheered. "Called it!"

Candy groaned, running a hand over her face. "Um, why are you guys here?"

Bailey smirked. "Don't worry, honey pie. We're here to make sure Lincoln treats you right." She turned to glare pointedly at Lincoln. "Not that he really has a choice."

Lincoln lifted his hands. "Understood."

Bailey leaned back, satisfied, then grabbed a cupcake from the tray. "Now, I say we celebrate. Patty's Cakes is thriving, Bradley is facing legal hell, and my best friend is disgustingly in love."

Candy opened her mouth to argue, but Lincoln beat her to it. "I'm comfortable with that phrasing."

Bailey nearly fell out of her chair, laughing. "Oh, I like you," she wheezed.

"Ugh, I hate you," Candy said, glancing between Lincoln's smug smile and her best friend.

"No, you love me," Bailey corrected.

Lincoln leaned in, voice low against Candy's ear. "You do love her."

"Unfortunately." Candy sighed dramatically, then whispered. "But, I love you, too."

He nuzzled her neck and whispered in her ear. "I love you, too, now try to get rid of them."

Candy shoved him lightly, laughing despite herself.

Fine.

Lincoln was doing what he did best—make plans—and she couldn't wait to get messy with him.

About Amber W. Lynne

An award-winning author from the misty, coffee-scented land-scapes of the Pacific Northwest, Amber blends slow-burn tension, heart-tugging emotion, and just the right amount of sweet and heat into every story she writes. The relationships are relatable and her heroines are fierce, independent, and (sometimes) a little stubborn, but they always find the right man to love them.

Fueled by caffeine and an unshakable belief in love, Amber has been crafting stories since childhood, drawn to the way romance can heal, challenge, and transform. When she's not writing, she's playing with her five kids (I KNOW!), helping fellow writers embrace their literary dreams, or spending time with her hubby making a love story of her own.

<u>Ways to stay in touch:</u>

- Subscribe to her Newsletter

- Via email: info@AmberWLynne.com

- Follow on Instagram - AmberLynne.Author

- Follow on Facebook - Amber W. Lynne, Author

Also by Amber W. Lynne

<u>**Working For Love**</u>

Lanyards & Lariats
Toolbelts & Ties
Spreadsheets & Sprinkles
Gowns & Gavels
Bourbons & Bling
Holly & Heartbeats

Leave a review at your favorite retailer, and sign-up for Amber's newsletter, to get more love stories, sneak peeks, a chance at Beta or ARC reads, and exclusive giveaways.

To find more books by Amber W. Lynne, visit:
https://amberlynneauthor.com

Gowns & Gavels

Working for Love, Book 4

The sequined hem threw off sparks of spotlight that danced like fire.

Taylor Preston sat in the front row of New York Fashion Week, her knees angled modestly, hands clasped so tightly they ached. Her gaze locked on the model striding down the runway.

The gown shimmered. Its silver and rose-gold threads caught the light in a rhythm so deliberate, it felt like watching poetry walking in heels.

Bailey leaned close, voice low and dry. "That one looks like she could conquer the world in stilettos and still send thank-you cards."

Candy grinned, biting into a pistachio macaron. "She looks like she'd drive that stiletto straight through the heart of the first man dumb enough to cross her. I wish I had the guts to wear clothes like that."

On Taylor's other side, Molly, ever composed, didn't smile, but lifted her sparkling water in agreement. "Three votes yes."

Taylor tried to follow their chattering conversation and remain present in the moment. "Candy, you could wear glitter every day if you wanted," she murmured, but her throat tightened, and her smile crumpled at the edges.

When the music shifted, another model glided past. She was draped in midnight blue tulle that whispered along the floor. The flared fabric draped at the hip in asymmetrical lines. Taylor's fingers twitched as if they held a pencil and were ready to trace the dress's flowing lines.

A detail on the next look tightened the muscles in her neck. It had beaded cuffs shaped like satin vines, winding upward from the wrist. She'd drawn that cuff. In a sunlit room she used to rent...years ago, when she still believed in the beauty of fashion more than the politics behind it.

Her past was wearing stilettos and striding down the runway.

"Favorite so far?" Bailey nudged.

Taylor blinked. "I...don't know. They blur together."

A lie. She remembered each one. Every line. Every curve. Every sketch scrawled into margins when she should've been working another shift. They were her lifeline then, built in stolen hours, clung to in rooms that smelled of mold and old carpet. To pretend otherwise was weak armor. To admit she was watching her dreams parade down the runway with someone else's name stitched to them...that was unbearable.

The show marched on, merciless. Chiffon trenches floated past like storm clouds. Heavy gowns glittered with beadwork so intricate she could almost feel the weight drag at her own shoulders. They were perfect. They were hers, and now, they were his.

Taylor clapped when she had to, palms striking without feeling. She refused to look at the program, refused to let her eyes land on the bold, confident font announcing the collection. His name would break her. Pretending not to see it was all she had left.

Then the last model appeared.

Everything stopped.

The blonde wore a pleated capelet shaped like butterfly wings. Wings Taylor had sketched while humming along to her mother's favorite opera in a swampy apartment, scissors dull against cheap fabric. The silhouette was unmistakable.

Taylor's breath stalled. Her hand pressed flat against her blouse as if pressure alone could keep her together, but inside, something tore. A rip that had started years ago, splitting open seam by seam under the floodlights.

Anger came first. Slow. Heavy. A betrayal that set her jaw hard.

Laurent Delacroix.

How dare he parade her gown—exactly as she'd conceived it—before New York Fashion Week? Without a single stitch of acknowledgment for her work?

She watched as the model pivoted at the end of the catwalk, the butterfly wings spreading, exaggerating the woman's movement. Taylor's hand fell to her lap, fingers curling into fists. He hadn't just stolen a sketch. He'd stolen her past. Her pride. Now, he was coasting off the very soul of her work while people sipped champagne and wrote little hearts beside his name in their stylists' notebooks.

And yet, it wasn't really a surprise. That's what made it worse. Somewhere inside, buried beneath layers of grief and self-doubt, she'd expected this. Laurent Delacroix didn't mentor prodigies—he consumed them. He brought them close, warmed his hands by the spark of their creativity, and then smothered them before they could even catch flame.

She'd once admired him. Once let herself believe his smile meant approval, and that the way he lingered over her seam work and studied her pleats meant he saw her vision.

He'd seen something, alright. He'd seen her worth, and then he'd waited for her to lose sight of it so he could take it for himself.

Her throat dried. Her vision tunneled. Applause surged around her. Flashes lit the edges of her sight. Reviewers whispered. Stylists scribbled. Taylor sat frozen.

When the music fell away and silence pressed in, she couldn't stay seated. Her body rose before her mind caught up, shame and disbelief blurring together.

She slipped into the aisle, careful not to stumble, arms trembling anyway. Sequined gowns brushed against her legs as she moved past champagne flutes and crossed ankles. She kept her eyes down. Couldn't speak. Couldn't let out the hot pressure burning its way to her throat.

She needed a way out.

A slit in the velvet curtain revealed stage lights. She pushed through.

Backstage hit like a slap. There were glaring fluorescent lights, racks of silver metal, hairspray clinging to the air, stylists barking over dryers. A machine in full motion. Taylor moved through it invisibly, threading past tulle and sequins.

She ducked behind a wall of plastic-wrapped cocktail gowns. Her shoulder clipped a rack, sending a lookbook clattering to the ground. She winced but didn't stop.

She needed a corner. A second to breathe.

Pressed flat against the drywall, between garment bags and a makeup mirror, she forced her back rigid, struggling to hold herself together.

Hot tears startled her. She wasn't crying—she refused to cry—but the prickling proof was there, blurring the mascara she'd so carefully applied only hours earlier. She swiped at her face with the heel of her palm, angry at how fast it had all fallen apart.

"Oh my God," she whispered. "It's happening."

Not the theft—she'd already known about that—but the remembering.

The way the hem of that final gown dragged something up from the dead. Her past unraveled like a ripped seam. Her old studio, her notebooks, the summer she'd given everything she had to an assignment she believed would make her career. She'd run away from it all, stayed quiet for years, and convinced herself that silence was smarter than going to war with Laurent Delacroix.

But sitting in that chair, watching her own work parade down the runway under someone else's spotlight? It broke the last remnants of her already cracked ego.

"Taylor?"

Candy's voice cut through.

Taylor's head snapped up as her friend rounded the corner,

wide-eyed, slowing when she saw the hiding spot.

"I—" Taylor's voice cracked. "I had to get out."

"Okay." Candy's brows knit. "What happened?"

Taylor's laugh came thin, dying almost instantly. "I didn't think it would hit like this. I thought I'd see him, see the similarities, feel bruised. Maybe jealous. Not—"

"An ex?"

"No. My old mentor." She didn't know how to explain to Candy how much he'd meant to her. He'd been more than a teacher, almost a father, and definitely done more damage than an ex. "He was the reason my life fell apart. It just—"

"Shattered?"

She nodded, eyes glossy again.

"It wasn't just a gown," she whispered. "It was my past. The dreams I boxed up. The sketches I told myself weren't worth keeping, and I realized...they didn't stay buried. He pulled them into the spotlight and took the applause, and I let him."

Candy stepped in beside her, quiet, holding out a tissue.

Taylor took it.

"I thought it would be okay. I've moved on!" she said, looking around. "But my past was here waiting for me."

AVAILABLE AT MAJOR BOOK RETAILERS

RECIPE: Brambleberry Tartlets

Candy & Bailey's Childhood Favorite!

Serves: 6–8
Prep Time: 30 min
Cook Time: 25–30 min

Inspired by *Spreadsheets & Sprinkles*, these Brambleberry Tartlets are a perfect balance of buttery, flaky crust and a luscious, tangy-sweet berry filling. The hint of citrus zest and vanilla bean makes them truly special.

INGREDIENTS:

For the Tart Crust:
- 1 ¼ cups (160g) all-purpose flour

- ½ cup (115g) unsalted butter, cold and cut into small cubes

- ¼ cup (30g) powdered sugar

- 1 egg yolk

- 1 tsp vanilla extract

- ½ tsp salt

- 1–2 tbsp ice-cold water

For the Brambleberry Filling:
- 1 cup (150g) fresh blackberries

- 1 cup (150g) fresh raspberries

- ½ cup (100g) granulated sugar

- 1 tbsp cornstarch

- 1 tsp lemon zest

- 1 tbsp lemon juice

- ½ tsp vanilla bean paste or extract

For the Whipped Cream Topping:
- ½ cup (120ml) heavy cream, chilled

- 1 tbsp powdered sugar

- ½ tsp vanilla bean paste or extract

INSTRUCTIONS:

Make the Tart Crust:

1. In a mixing bowl, combine flour, powdered sugar, and salt.

2. Add the cold butter cubes and use a pastry cutter (or your fingers) to work them into the flour until it resembles coarse sand with pea-sized bits of butter.

3. In a small bowl, whisk together the egg yolk and vanilla extract. Pour into the flour mixture and gently mix.

4. Add ice water, 1 tablespoon at a time, until the dough just comes together when pinched between your fingers.

5. Form the dough into a disk, wrap in plastic wrap, and chill for at least 30 minutes.

6. Preheat oven to 375°F (190°C). Roll out the chilled dough on a lightly floured surface to ⅛-inch thickness.

7. Cut into circles and press gently into greased mini tartlet pans. Prick the bottoms with a fork.

8. Bake for 12-15 minutes, until lightly golden. Let cool completely.

Prepare the Brambleberry Filling:

1. In a small saucepan over medium heat, combine black-berries, raspberries, sugar, and cornstarch. Stir continuously.

2. Add lemon juice, zest, and vanilla bean paste. Cook for 5-7 minutes, stirring, until thickened and glossy.

3. Remove from heat and let cool slightly before spooning into the cooled tart crusts.

Make the Whipped Cream Topping:

1. In a large mixing bowl, beat heavy cream, powdered sugar, and vanilla bean paste until soft peaks form.

2. Pipe or spoon a small dollop onto each tartlet.

3. Garnish with extra lemon zest or fresh berries if desired. Can be served chilled or at room temperature.

Enjoy your own taste of Patty's Cakes and feel like a contender in the Sweet Success competition!

RECIPE: Cream Cheese Buttermilk Biscuits

An in a pinch twist on an old favorite!

Makes: 8-10 Biscuits
Prep Time: 15 min
Cook Time: 15 min

Created in the heat of competition after her sourdough starter was stolen, these cream cheese buttermilk biscuits rose golden and layered. Brushed with honey-butter, they proved simple ingredients could still hold their own under pressure.

INGREDIENTS:

- 2 cups all-purpose flour (or substitute 1 tbsp with

cornstarch for extra tenderness)

- 1 tbsp baking powder

- ½ tsp baking soda

- 1 tsp salt

- 1 tbsp sugar (optional, for a slight sweetness)

- 4 tbsp unsalted butter, cold and cubed

- 2 oz cream cheese, cold and cubed

- ¾ cup buttermilk, cold

- 1 tbsp melted butter (for brushing)

INSTRUCTIONS:

1. Preheat oven to 425°F (220°C). Line a baking sheet with parchment paper.

2. In a large bowl, whisk together flour, cornstarch (if using), baking powder, baking soda, salt, and sugar.

3. Using a pastry cutter (or your fingers), cut in the butter and cream cheese until the mixture resembles coarse crumbs with pea-sized bits of fat.

4. Gradually stir in the cold buttermilk until the dough just comes together. Be careful not to overmix!

5. Turn the dough onto a lightly floured surface and gently pat it into a rectangle, about ¾-inch thick. Fold the dough in half, rotate, and repeat 3 times to create layers.

6. Cut biscuits using a floured round cutter or knife. Press straight down—don't twist!

7. Place biscuits on the prepared baking sheet so they slightly touch (helps them rise taller).

8. Bake for 12–15 minutes or until golden brown.

9. Brush with melted butter and serve warm!

Enjoy your flaky, tender, and slightly tangy biscuits!

RECIPE: Lavender Honey Patty Cake

Candy & Lincoln's Prize-Winning Recipe

Serves: 6–8
Prep Time: 15 min
Cook Time: 25–30 min

This is the elevated version of Candy's mother's patty cake—the one that beat Bradley and reclaimed her family's legacy. The delicate floral notes of lavender blend with the deep richness of honey, vanilla, and browned butter, creating a cake that's timeless, heartfelt, and completely hers.

INGREDIENTS:

For the Cake:
- 2 ½ cups all-purpose flour

- 2 ½ tsp baking powder

- ½ tsp salt

- ¾ cup unsalted butter, browned and cooled

- ¾ cup honey

- ½ cup granulated sugar

- 3 large eggs

- 1 ½ tsp pure vanilla extract

- 1 cup whole milk

- 1 tbsp dried culinary lavender, finely ground

- 1 tsp lemon zest

For the Honey Lavender Glaze:
- 1 cup powdered sugar

- 2 tbsp honey

- 1 tbsp whole milk

- ½ tsp dried culinary lavender, finely ground

For Garnish:
- Fresh lavender sprigs (optional, for decoration)

- A light drizzle of honey

INSTRUCTIONS:

Step 1: Brown the Butter

- In a saucepan over medium heat, melt the butter. Stir continuously as it foams, then turns golden brown with a nutty aroma (about 3-4 minutes).

- Remove from heat and let it cool slightly.

Step 2: Prepare the Dry Ingredients

- In a mixing bowl, whisk together the flour, baking powder, salt, and ground lavender.

- Add the lemon zest and mix evenly to distribute the flavors.

Step 3: Whip the Wet Ingredients

- In another large bowl, beat the honey, sugar, and browned butter until smooth and slightly whipped.

- Add the eggs one at a time, beating after each addition. Stir in vanilla extract.

- Alternately mix in the dry ingredients and milk, beginning and ending with the dry ingredients. Mix until just combined—don't overmix!

Step 4: Bake to Perfection

- Preheat oven to 350°F (175°C). Grease a 9-inch round cake pan (or cupcake tins for mini versions!).

- Pour the batter into the prepared pan. Smooth the batter evenly.

- Bake for 28-32 minutes (or 18-20 minutes for cupcakes), until the top is golden and a toothpick comes out clean.

- Let the cake cool completely before glazing.

Step 5: Make the Honey Lavender Glaze
- Whisk together powdered sugar, honey, milk, and ground lavender until smooth and pourable.

- Drizzle the glaze over the cooled cake, letting it cascade down the sides.

- If desired, garnish with fresh lavender sprigs and a delicate drizzle of honey.

Slice, serve, and savor the taste of victory!